Praise for

Summer Cannibals

"Melanie Hobson writes with the dark energy and twisted exuberance reminiscent of her most celebrated predecessors—Atwood, Murdoch, Oates, and so many others plumbing the raw, violent depths of toxic families. Her mesmerizing characters are semi-feral, trapped and struggling under the terrible weight of what a man can do to a girl, a daughter, a wife. *Summer Cannibals* seems perfectly written for the world today, our blind greedy stumble from thing to thing."
—Bob Shacochis, author of *The Woman Who Lost Her Soul*

"Dark, risky, and as gorgeous as the ocean at midnight, Hobson's exquisitely written debut gathers a fractured grown family together for six dangerous days of lust, longing, sex, secrets, and stunning betrayals. The story may be set in the languid days of summer, but My God, it's a terrific scorcher."
—Caroline Leavitt, author of *Is This Tomorrow*

"There is a quality to Melanie Hobson's writing that reminds me of *Brideshead Revisited* or certain John Cheever stories; a quality of languid lyricism and moral corruption that I found immediately arresting. The story of three sisters carrying out both subtle and shocking acts of deceit and desire (And oh, Pippa!) is something to be savored like a gin and tonic on a summer afternoon by the lake. But a storm is rolling in and the water, moments ago so inviting and glorious, begins to grow dark. Is it safe? Should you dive in? *Summer Cannibals* announces the arrival of a great talent that book clubs and reviewers alike will adore."
—Matt Bondurant, author of *The Night Swimmer*

Summer Cannibals

Melanie Hobson

Black Cat
New York

First published in Canada in 2018 by Penguin Random House

First Grove Atlantic edition: September 2018

Printed in the United States of America

ISBN 978-0-8021-2852-2
eISBN 978-0-8021-4652-6

Black Cat
an imprint of Grove Atlantic
154 West 14th Street
New York, NY 10011

Distributed by Publishers Group West

groveatlantic.com

18 19 20 10 9 8 7 6 5 4 3 2 1

For Charlie,
Aidan & Phoebe.

And for my sisters:
Helen, Megan, Imogen, Elizabeth, Fleur.

Summer Cannibals

Thursday

1

The house had its way of holding them. Their father liked to tell how he'd bought it with a credit card—a cash advance to make up the ten percent needed for the deposit—and it seemed as equally and gloriously ridiculous, that this should all be theirs. That first day, after the papers were signed, the sisters had run laughing and shrieking through the house with its three floors, two staircases, seven bedrooms and all the rest— living, dining, family, library, kitchen, butler's pantry, bathrooms, hallways, passageways and entryways. They explored and claimed rooms and then just as quickly relinquished them as they found another and another, shouting that they were lost, crying out that they'd found "the best thing ever," bare feet thudding up and down, up and down, across and over. Doors slammed. Drawers were pulled open and locks fiddled with. The old laundry chute was discovered and heads were put through the small doors on each landing that let into it as they prodded each other, but none of them were brave enough to go to the chute's terminus in the basement. That rough stone-walled basement the original builders had dynamited from the solid limestone of the escarpment the house was perched on. Beyond the house's walls, at the base of that cliff, was the city—gridded to the enormous lake like a mesh to keep the jutting land, and all it supported, from tumbling down.

I can't hear the children, their father had said, looking at his wife triumphantly. This house swallows them.

They were leaning on the metal fence at the cliff's edge, the whole world spread out in front of them, and anyone would think these parents too young to have all this. That something was wrong; a mistake. But they knew that this was nothing less than what they deserved: the five acres of parkland which they would turn into exquisite gardens to surround the grand house with a landscape to match it in size and manner—this had always been owed to them. They were a couple whom people referred to as 'handsome' and it suited them because they resonated good breeding and all that went with it: high birth, property, education, bloodlines you could trace back to royalty. They were handsome and they knew it to be true, and theirs was a world that rewarded such things. David and Margaret Blackford were exactly where they were meant to be—at the dead end of a private lane you could drive by without noticing because the newer, smaller houses of the neighbourhood acted like a palisade of brick and mortar to keep the riff-raff out. The lane's three big houses were dealt in along the cliff's edge, a vestige from a time when it had all been fields and the founding families of that region had built their houses on the escarpment's very brow. This view had always been worth braving the winter gales that howled up off the lake and even then, in the early century, the occupants knew the defensible value of a horizon.

At the lane's entrance, where it met the ordinary street, was a bulging masonry wall behind which was a cloistered convent: a rundown mysterious place their father forbade them from entering. Even the name of the convent terrified: Sisters of the Precious Blood. Their father, who rarely noticed what his girls whispered about and even more rarely took an interest in it, had—with that single restriction—made the place irresistible. In the years to come, one of the nuns would take daily walks up and down the lane from the convent to the family's driveway and back again, having taken a vow of silence and contemplation. And the girls would tempt her, with their father's encouragement, because he saw the nun's appearance at his property line for what it was: a trespass. They would lounge near the gate on their bicycles and then speed out to intercept, shouting hellos, riding circles, going no-hands, skidding their tires, trying to get her to respond. Doing everything short of touching her as she walked in an eddy of robes like a villain from a comic book, her presence making the vampire crypts and legions of undead seem more likely than ever. And when the sun would go down the girls would scramble to shut their bedroom windows, even on the hottest nights, afraid she'd come for them. As if she were the greatest threat to their security, their little paradise. The only person they had to fear.

Their driveway, where the nun turned, was defined by two stone pillars which were knocked over regularly by the garbage truck and snowplow. The drivers piled the wreckage back up at new and eccentric angles in a sneering indictment of this fancy house with its crude gateposts that deserved to be bulldozed because maybe then the rich bastards would put up something appropriate, like electric gates with a keypad to come and go. A code they'd have to be trusted with. It was only the cases of beer at Christmastime—put out on the porch steps to freeze overnight—that stopped them from leaving the blocks where they fell. Instead of a metal gate, the girls' father used an old sawhorse to block the property's entrance from the regular snoopers who liked to just barely roll their cars along the lane and down the long drive as though this were their right—to take in the acres of gardens and the orchestrated countryside at a crawl, stopping to exclaim over new blooms or a shrub's lush foliage when their selfsame shrub back at their modest home was still bare. As if that was treason. Just another betrayal to add to their list of grievances against these upstarts who took and kept everything for themselves. The gawkers would stop at the house and look around contemptuously before turning to inch back out, trawling for every shred of evidence to justify their position that here, without question, was the rot underpinning the nation's decay.

The girls' father believed that the simple wooden sawhorse he placed at the gate, with his own hands, was a denial of that judgment that wealth begat indolence because there was something practical and self-reliant about that barrier. And it fit perfectly, he would say, with the Georgian style of the house which echoed gentle country living and turnstiles, fox hunts and steeplechases, noblesse oblige, even though (their mother would remark) this was Hamilton, Canada—a town founded in the monstrous flickering shadows of the steel mills on the southern shore of Lake

Ontario. A place where at night, deep in the east end, you could see the climbing flames firing the stack that spewed soot onto the narrow red brick houses in the adjacent streets, coating them, Blakean. This was Hamilton, a workers' town.

They were sisters: Georgina, Jacqueline and Philippa. Adults now, and with families of their own, but the youngest, Pippa, was sick. Eight months pregnant with her fifth, she'd left her husband and four children in New Zealand and was coming here. The others were coming home too. More than three decades had passed since they'd run through the house on that first day, and there'd been days—too many to count—when the house had sat hard and unloved within its ruffle of green grass and hedge and flower. When the sky was dull and grey and the windows reflected bleakness, all flat and giving nothing back, and it seemed a place of such uncompromising severity that its stone walls would let nothing in or out. And then some mornings, it would rise with the sun and display the warmth inherent in its blocks and the glass would gleam and the garden, that lush profusion, would reflect inward to the rooms and fill the house with life. Figures would move from window to window as though it were a dance and they partnered with the air. And it was on those days that the world was right and days were measured in increments of joy. It was all there was and would ever be. It was family.

2

No one could see David back there in the tangle of rose bushes and if it hadn't been for the fact of the roses themselves, and all the money and time that had gone into raising them, he would have pissed right where he was. Total privacy. Instead, he went back to the far corner under the oak where they piled small trimmings and windfall and other incidental cleanups to decompose. It was his usual spot—adding his own waste to that of the garden.

Urinating outside was, he supposed, a harmless predilection of his, and the older he got the more enjoyable it became. He unzipped his shorts and pulled his penis out just enough not to wet himself, and watched the sputtering arc splash against the leaves of the dead hosta he'd put there the day before. Relief as his bladder emptied. Not everyone ends up pissing themselves, he thought proudly. He practised stopping and restarting the stream of urine. No trouble at all. He shook himself off, zipped his shorts back up . . . but something didn't seem right. What was it? and then he realized. It was the sound of liquid splashing nearby. But not from him. And then he saw. His neighbour, in the small house that abutted the back end of David's property, was rinsing out a cooler with a hose. The man was barefoot and bare chested and wearing track pants, and with his long, unkempt hair it was no wonder he was out of work. No legitimate employer would want to look at that every day. The rhododendrons had grown up high enough along the back fence that there was a chance the neighbour hadn't seen and that David could just melt away back to the roses without being noticed, but when he moved the man looked up and grinned right at him through the branches. No embarrassment, just a look that said *Yeah, mate. Who's the lout now, eh?* Was that a thumbs-up he was giving him? David thought he read an invitation to come by for a beer, as if all it took was an act of public nudity to put them on a level playing field. As if David, with that single indiscretion, had reduced himself to a layabout with nothing better to do than ready a cooler for another case of beer. As if semi-retirement and uselessness were one and the same and they were in it together, a band of brothers arrayed against the collective indignity of being home instead of out there, on the battlefield, among men.

Fucker, David muttered.

That helped. Made him feel dangerous again. Made him feel he was stalking something, like a leopard slinking through the undergrowth. *Yes*, David thought. He was a leopard. Fast and sleek and vicious, and whatever crossed him, he'd crush and digest it and shit it back out. Amend the soil.

Fucking cunt, he swore a little louder. Moving away, return-ing to the roses now that he'd made his point. Now that he was invincible again, had marked his territory, had staked his claim. Now that he was out of reach. And how easily then the man was forgotten and became something, a mild irritation, just back there in the foliage. A half-formed rumour from beyond the known world; David back in his realm again. More than enough here, he thought, to concern myself with. The garden not the least of it.

The rose bed—David stared down at it dejectedly—was full of weeds again. He'd mulched the whole thing at the beginning of the summer but he should have insisted on weed cloth when they'd first been planted thirty-five years ago. He thought about this every time he worked out there because every time he stooped and got close to the ground, like he did now, he saw the vast legions of invading dock and chickweed, even dandelion, making inroads everywhere. He'd never get it sorted before the garden tour, which was only two days away. The best he could manage, he decided, was to weed the first twelve inches in from the edge and trust that no one looked beyond that. Fortunately, the roses had been mostly finished for a month, so David knew that would be in his favour. Not many people, he thought, will stop to consider the few hundred straggling blooms that were left; not when there were so many other beds rife with colour. This will become, he reasoned, a sort of passageway they'll use between spectacles. A place of undeniable beauty, yes—who could argue with that—but not somewhere to linger. Rather, somewhere to build your strength back up before the next marvel knocks you flat again. David liked to think of these grounds as an enormous series of interconnecting rooms with such wealth on display that it rivalled the Winter Palace—but was of course better, because it had none of the baroque gaudiness he found so undignified. And, it was his.

He knew his wife had reservations about the timing of this tour but he was the one who worked the garden now, not her, and he knew there was still much to excite a group of enthusiasts. There was the huge circular garden in front of the house with its embroidery parterre in colour combinations so vibrant and varied that it looked, truly, like the work of a hundred hands and a thousand lengths of thread, the intricate gravel paths between the beds like seams joining them together. All told, it was ninety feet across and still fully in bloom. The white garden off the terrace was still blanketed with flowers, and the shaded woodland areas were broken by patches of sunlight revealing late gentians and trefoils mixed with asters, daisies and ladies' tresses—and even some wildflowers the birds had seeded, which David hadn't noticed until that morning. Pale blues like the sky—something else the garden had gifted him. There was the topiary, of course, and the cutting garden and herbaceous border, and there were still masses of rhododendrons and azaleas blooming to set off the wintergreen and ferns and primulas they were planted among. Every turn, David thought triumphantly, will bring a surprise. Too many for even him to count. If only his wife were as attentive as he was, she'd see that too and stop meddling. If only she minded better.

Like every job in the garden, the staking—why he'd gone out there in the first place—had morphed into something else. But that's the way it always was and he wasn't complaining. The

11

longer he stayed out there the better, because inside his wife would be colluding with Georgina, and by late tonight, Pippa and Jax would be there too. Women. He supposed he was resigned to them. To small instances being stretched into tragedies and every sinew of the monster being examined and picked apart. He'd learned just to shut up and go away, and this solution suited everyone. When he'd married, marriage was the only way to have limitless sex without risks, and so like a pill he'd swallowed it. And everyone else was doing it too. Weddings, for several years, replaced dinner-and-movie nights and then there were children and christenings and the whole juggernaut of family milestones, and the sex, he discovered too late, lessened as all those other activities multiplied. It was a sour deal, really, and a secretive one. His father must've known but didn't say anything, just clapped him on the shoulder as though he was proud when what it really meant was "Welcome to the Shithouse, son." And then the babies had all been girls, which had only hurt him even more. Life, he often thought, was a never-ending fight for virility.

David picked up one of the bamboo stakes at his feet and threaded it through a sprawling rose bush to help steady it. Thinking about that, about having been cheated. About having been marginalized, a minority. *Shit*, he'd forgotten the staking ties. This morning wasn't starting well at all. He didn't even know where those garden ties were. If he couldn't find them he'd have to buy some, which would mean another fight with his wife because he never came away from the nursery without a trunk full of plants and lately she'd been talking about making the garden smaller and more manageable for the two of them. Every few years she went through a phase like this, her "third-world jag" he called it, where she said they had too much and everyone else too little and shouldn't they simplify. No, he'd shout at her, we shouldn't. I've worked hard for this. *Slaved* for it. And it's not as if, he'd finish, throwing his arms out to make his point, whirling like a dust devil, we can send everything over to Africa. And why would they want it? They'd just ruin a silk rug on those dirt floors and any artwork would be lost on them. It takes a thousand years of prosperity, he'd yell, *a thousand years!* to understand Michelangelo, and you can forget about Tintoretto or Van Gogh. They're still trying to keep basic things like toilets going or even just a fucking roof to protect themselves from that god-awful sun. And who would *choose* to live in a place that hot?? They have to take a little responsibility for *that*. No—clean water's the stage they're at, he'd say when his wife started up. I doubt they even have four walls.

He suspected her of taking boxes of their possessions to local charities when he wasn't looking but he couldn't prove it, because the truth was that a truckload of items could be removed from their house every month and the difference would be so slight as to be imperceptible. She was always rearranging things anyway, so he'd given up trying to keep a count.

David rummaged through the shelves in the coach house, looking for the coil of plastic wire he'd used only a few weeks ago on the hollyhocks. He could feel his temper rising. Bloody typical, he muttered. Shambles. Too much to ask, isn't it, for something to break my way. And then he saw it, the green twist of it, back behind the shears where he'd hidden it from his grandson who, as a toddler, had liked to unspool it and leave trails for the lawnmower to run over. David still hid it as a

13

matter of course, just in case. As if Georgina's son, at twelve years old, might start playing with it again.

I don't know why, he thought, glancing down at the house as he crossed the drive and re-entered the roses, they can't be more like me. I should have insisted on it. Fathers—he stretched the wire out and cut the length he needed, his breathing beginning to level out—should have some say in how their kids end up. Somehow, we should be in charge of it. We would get the results we're looking for, even with only girls.

His penis nestled up against his leg.

That family, he thought peevishly, looking in the direction of the house, doesn't know what's good for them. He'd given them all that they had and they'd repaid him by taking it without a single word of thanks and now—he bent to the roses again—they were trying to sabotage him by making their supposed crises collide with the one thing, the *one thing* he wanted for himself—this garden tour.

The newspaper that Margaret had open on her lap was completely still. Not even the suggestion of a breeze to flutter it. It was going to be hot. Humid too, she guessed. At least they might get a thunderstorm out of it. The garden could use the water. She pushed her hair back from her face, both hands massaging her scalp, sweating, and lit another cigarette. Letting the smoke find its own way out, a veil across her face, disappearing along her scalp, feathering through her hair like steam. Not that rain, she thought, will be enough to fix the mess in time for his stupidity. She hadn't gardened for years—he'd finally succeeded in that—but she could still see every last inch of her creation as if she were moving through it, and she knew that this late in the season too many of the plants were making their preparations for the coming snows and it was all out of balance, listing toward dormancy, and would require a level of imagination that she knew the tourists wouldn't have.

The lake's northern edge was smeared out of existence by the rising heat, but it was enough for Margaret to see the city's buildings giving way to the near shore. She could imagine the rest. She'd stared at it often enough, years and years of it, that she could, with her eyes shut, rebuild the entire thing block by stone by tile and she could press it between the pages of one of her books and do it again and again as often as was necessary to make it real. In a room upstairs she had stacks of books like that—collages and assemblages where she put the world in its place. An inventory of everything that mattered. My own private garden, she thought spitefully.

When the children were little they used to sit, all together, at the kitchen table with sliding piles of coloured paper and shoeboxes filled with crayons and markers and bottles of glue, cutting and sticking and stamping and creating masterpiece after masterpiece for display. For the fridge, for the wall, for an envelope sent to their Gran in Toronto. For peace and quiet in a house ruled by voices, each one louder than the one before. The children outgrew it, or turned their backs on it, or fidgeted too much—but Margaret never did. And with whole sections of department stores being turned into shelves of scrapbooking supplies no one ever thought it strange: she was just another housewife making a memory chain, a modern tapestry, a shadow box out of her life. Another made-up activity to give some structure to her day.

But Margaret's were different. They were secret. They were riddles and conundrums. They were a feast of materials and impressions all layered and woven together so that if one of the girls or David were to look, they wouldn't understand what they were looking at, not really. *Abstract* is what Georgina would probably label it. These collages of Margaret's were a way to slow things down and sort and itemize. To take the unruly mess and give it shape and permanence. And if what she ended up with was contoured and rough then that's what it was, not her fault. She just put it down as it came. She secured it as it was.

But this . . . She stared at the lake now, the whole blinding flatness of it, its distance and breadth and the tedium of its colour. What could she do with this . . . with Pippa, the coming baby, and everyone flooding home to her. How could she catalogue all of that? And now her husband, in what she knew was a fit of arrogance—for he was always striving to best and outmanoeuvre her—had invited the barbarian hordes in to ravage what was left of her beautiful garden.

Margaret settled back onto the chaise longue, legs stretched out and trimly put together, her dressing gown discreetly tucked. God she was tired. Since Pippa had phoned two days ago and asked to come home, Margaret had only slept in patches. She saw her husband's deep sleeps as a kind of betrayal. Just another example of his overall cruelty. She turned and looked out at the dogwood and the swathe of tradescantia and knew David was out there somewhere, primping the garden for this ridiculous tour, which he'd organized without consulting her because he knew she would've put a stop to it. It was August, when the garden was at its worst, and she would have told him that no one who knew anything about gardens would pay to see this end-of-season tangle of faded blooms. This tour was bound to be a failure. Normally, she'd encourage that for him—any chance to take him down a notch or two—but with Pippa coming home and the upheaval that would already bring . . .

As Margaret looked, he crossed the drive and went into the coach house. He'll have forgotten something, she thought. He'll come down here and ask me where it is. Something he's misplaced, he will blame on me.

She leaned back, letting her cigarette burn down, thinking about cakes. She'd have to put the fruit on to boil, check there was enough butter, measure the sugar, clean a pan if it wasn't clean already. Had she washed it after the last one she'd made? He'll probably eat this one too. The cakes weren't for him but like everything she did, he assumed they were.

Taking bites out of me for years.

There he was, coming out again. She saw him look at the house before disappearing back into the landscape and she knew that look. It was the coronation look that fastened the Imperial Robe of silk and ermine about his shoulders and St. Edward's Crown upon his head . . . the look that made them all courtiers. And it was the look that would gaze at everything she'd made and see nothing. *None of it at all.* Except what he claimed by the Divine Right of Kings. *Which was all.*

Margaret lit another cigarette off the old one and tucked the packet in against her leg. Her family hadn't approved of David, although his medical licence and the income it signalled did, at least, make him viable. Better than some of the other derelicts this only child of theirs had entertained. And there was—*thank God*—the useful fact that he hailed from Stratford which was something they could work with, massaging the details so that by the time the marriage was inevitable it was understood by everyone who mattered that his pedigree was delicately aligned with Shakespeare himself. They'd used the same modus operandi with their business—a company that supplied food to airlines, finessing that mundane but obscenely lucrative service into a social currency that had made them one of the most prominent philanthropic families in Toronto. Their names were on concert halls and galleries and on major donor lists for the ballet and the theatre and the distinguished all-girls private school Margaret had attended, going to classes in a building with her family name on it. All those advantages, and yet she'd fallen for a boy well outside their orbit.

It's not that we think he's *wrong* for you, her mother had explained. We just think he isn't *right*.

Their meeting had been pure chance. The hospital where David was doing his residency was in the same city as the university where Margaret was taking art classes—a pretty collection of buildings with enough prestige to balance out their high acceptance rates. Even so, their paths would never have crossed if that hospital hadn't been the laughingstock of all the other older medical establishments in Canada because of its innovative programs like hanging original artwork outside the rooms of terminal patients to "heal and give their families a way back to life." David's rotation in oncology coincided with Margaret's artwork having been selected by a committee. It was her first show, and she was giddy with having won the chance to display her canvases, which were docile landscapes in miniature—hay bales and farmhouses and hillsides mostly—and painted in oils so thick she'd applied them with palette knives. An Old World richness, she hoped, at odds with the antiseptic meanness of the hospital. Something safe but voluptuous.

Very nice, he'd said from behind her as she reached both arms up over her head to hang a canvas of a plow. She'd decided to place it high because she knew it was her least successful, and she'd only included it to round her exhibit out to the required ten.

Cheeky, she'd thought, turning around to see who'd said that and noting the quick flick of his eyes up to her face from what—she guessed rightly—was her bottom. It should have incensed her but there was something about his steady cockiness that made her flirt back. Something teasing and attractive and new, something dangerous, which fit perfectly into her view of herself just then as a creative force with unbridled appetites. That very night they'd lain on her narrow bed before going out to dinner, Margaret quizzing him on her anatomy and David holding her down and tracing it with his teeth.

Birds of a feather, he'd smiled as he gnawed on her breastbone.

He was older, but she'd already given up on the boys her age. She'd tried, over and over, but always found them too timid, too circumspect. She'd decided that what she needed was a Diego Rivera—and she'd found him in David, she thought. Someone out of the ordinary who would provoke her artistic nature into creating works of magnificence.

You're a goad, she'd said gleefully as he mounted her.

Yes! he'd cried. A goat! A randy goat.

But a doctor's wife, she discovered after she'd married him, couldn't paint pictures of vaginas rupturing and expect them to be hung in the public domain. Only her husband, she discovered, had the rights to that.

She'd had to find another way.

And so the collages and the children and the difficult husband and the house and the gardens. It was really, Margaret thought, curling her toes back and feeling a surge of pride, I who've arranged all of this. A maelstrom to keep her world spinning.

3

Georgina placed the secateurs at the monkshood's stem. She ran them down a few feet and snapped through, brutal and efficient, a faint ooze of blood trailing across her fingers where the blade had pinched them. The bloom was a faded almost cobalt blue, starting to brown, but she'd use it anyway. She'd just make the rest up—the freshness, the gloss, the colour so saturated it hit you full on . . . wasn't that what she did, after all—make things up? Wasn't that her role as an associate professor of art history? She whacked at another stem. *The artist meant this, the artist meant that, the artist was copying, emulating, paying homage to . . .* all just a con job. *And what about me?* she thought, sweeping her eyes across the perennials. Monet had his precious lilies and enough water to drown himself in, Gauguin had all the flesh and the dogs, and Picasso his masks and Van Gogh with his goddamn razor blade and I, I have—. She jabbed at a daisy. This. No spectacle in that. Like a print on a schoolgirl's dress.

Along the gravel path at the border's rear there were weeds pushing up everywhere and the hollyhocks, some of them, were nearly horizontal. Someone had begun staking them, she could see that, but had only made it a third of the way and of the remainder, the outsized flower heads were winning. She chopped the few plume poppies still blooming, some phlox, coneflowers, rudbeckia, shastas until she had an immense armful she could split between all the bedrooms. There'd even be enough for her parents' room, and she knew they were going to need that added fragrance because the air passing between them ever since Georgina had arrived was acrid, and bound to get worse. This garden tour, she knew from experience, had all the hallmarks of a calamity.

Hefting the flowers onto her hip the way you'd hold a child, Georgina paused to watch a bee fly through and land on a bloom and flit away immediately, as if it knew the flower was dead and not worth the effort. As if the pollen shrivelled to nothing when it was cut, lost its usefulness, its taste—all in the last ten minutes. Did bees have a sense of taste? She doubted it, but she doubted a lot of things. Wasn't her whole life guided by that? Everything elevated for scrutiny. Georgina lifted a sandal and tipped it, releasing a rivulet of little stones that had been trapped there. She looked up at the house and saw the ivy creeping up to the eaves and digging into the mortar between the stones, pulling the paint loose. Beginning to smother her bedroom window. They'll need to find someone to trim it back, she thought, remembering what her mother had told her about the man who'd trimmed it the last eighteen autumns. That he'd broken his back in a fall the previous spring and, her mother had declared as she threw her hands out in exasperation, refuses to climb a ladder now. Even a *step*stool. As if he had no right to caution, no good reason to leave them so completely in the lurch. As if her family and this house must always be taken into account. That they were the control group the rest of the world was measured against. The foundation for everything; the template for all there was.

Georgina supposed that the ivy, too, would be something they'd task her with.

She cut across the grass and went in the front door, thinking her mother might be on the porch by now and that going in this way might buy her a little time before her mother started interfering, because Georgina wanted all the pleasure of arranging the bouquets for herself. Her own garden wasn't much more than a few self-sustaining shrubs and a wash of yellowing ferns underneath a couple of poplar trees. There were no cutting gardens, or really much of anything. She dropped the flowers into a pile next to the sink, the mass of them spreading out across the sugar bowl and the round tin of tea bags and the old pewter bowl her parents collected their food scraps in. The kitchen was bright, the rising sunlight flooding it, and Georgina felt a lightening of her spirit as if some unpleasantness had been avoided and she could relax and enjoy just being there in the moment, by herself, under the cascading beauty of a fine summer day and these frothy waves of petals.

Hello, darling.

Margaret had come in quietly, reaching past her daughter to fill the kettle.

Mind if I just— The hollyhocks are over, aren't they?

Georgina stepped aside while her mother ran water into the kettle, claiming that sink with all the years and the meals she'd cooked and all the judgments she'd laid down among her children to keep their squabbles from drawing blood.

I don't know what your father was thinking, arranging a tour at this time of year. And his first one too.

Margaret reached for a tea bag, readying her cup with a third of a teaspoon of sugar, leaving the spoon in, drawing her dressing gown more tightly across her chest. Patterned blue paisley satin that was unravelling but she wore it anyway. She started picking up the flowers, stripping their stems.

Did he talk to you about it? Before he booked it?

It was an innocent enough question, conversational, but Georgina knew it was more than that. Her mother was trying to determine the extent of the enemy. How best to counterattack.

I'll get another vase, Georgina said rather than answering, going into the next room and getting the putty-white one from the mantel.

They're for the bedrooms, Georgina told her mother when she came back, putting down the small vase that she'd brought and lifting the big glass one out of the sink before her mother could stuff any more flowers into it. Her mood was already souring, the kitchen beginning to feel small with herself and her mother in it.

When does Jax get in? Georgina asked, manoeuvring herself carefully back in front of the sink so her mother couldn't reach the flowers or the vase, looking at what was left to work with— yellow rudbeckia, one short phlox and two longer ones, and a confusion of different-coloured poppies. None of which would look good together.

Oh. Late. Midnight, something like that. I told her, take a taxi from the airport, I'll pay for it.

As if Jax doesn't have a wallet.

Where's your father? she asked then, in that way she had of making impatience sound like indifference. Practised over years and years. I suppose I'll have to make another cake, she said, frowning at what was left of the one she'd made the other day. Crumbs, mostly. It hadn't even stayed around long enough for Margaret to shake the icing sugar across its top or transfer it to a plate from the butcher's block where she'd knocked it out of the pan to cool.

Georgina shrugged. She could tell her mother was looking for a fight and she wasn't going to give it to her. Bad enough she was there at all instead of at her own house, working, which was what she was supposed to be doing, which was why she'd put James in sailing camp so she could prepare her syllabi and her lectures and finish the article she'd promised to have ready a month ago. *Bullshit*, Georgina said under her breath, cramming the flowers into the two vases. She wasn't going to let this get to her. She was an adult and a mother too, she thought, looking out past the cliff to the lake. James, her son, was down there somewhere sulking. Somewhere at the blunted edge of all those streets.

We don't even get on the water until the last day, he'd shrieked before slamming the car door that morning. The very last *day*.

Georgina had read about this in the newspaper, early puberty, but she thought it only affected the girls. Just another thing, she thought, where he's different. Another aberration on my plate—feeling increasingly sorry for herself, stuck there in her childhood kitchen. She stood still a moment, hands on the vase's neck, her mother working on her tea, and she looked over the lake toward the boomerang of escarpment on the other side. It was hazy, the heat already rising from the highway and running along its base into Toronto, where everything she longed for happened. There was too much smog to see it properly but she knew it was there and stuffed with life, its downtown stacked to the sky, the single gold tower of the Royal Bank gleaming like an ingot. It was always there, just far enough away to be beyond her reach. If this house was a country seat, then Toronto was a walled palace where the brightest minds lived under the patronage of a populace who could never get enough. Were always hungry for improvements, discoveries, magnum opuses. A productive riot of creativity and innovation. While out here in the provinces, Georgina thought defeatedly, we're still rotating the same crops year after year after fucking year. Even her grandparents had never seen her as someone who might, one day, benefit from their civic largesse. As if her last name—her father's name—didn't have the necessary brass to do anything original. The one thing we'll give you credit for, Georgina had once overheard her grandparents tell her father, is that you didn't indulge Margaret's artistic pretensions.

Georgina shifted her eyes to the harbour and the few boats wallowing slack-sailed offshore and thought of James again. She had to stop feeling sorry for him. Daycare, preschool, after-school—yes, she'd done that to him, started him at four months old, but hadn't she chosen them well? Programs that got him outside? Not overcrowded single rooms with locks on the door and the same grubby toys year after year, young teachers who were just killing time until someone married them and set them up in their own homes. And that sailing camp had a waiting list that went over to a second page. Georgina had had to pull strings to get him in. She'd hired an occupational therapist to work out his kinks, manipulate his motor skills, brush his arms to organize his sensory input. Wasn't she doing everything she could?

He could use a little neglect, she thought. Some time away from her. She'd promised her mother she'd stay and look after Pip, just the sisters, no other family pressing in on them. It was their mother's idea of a treatment plan. Gather us all together, like a school of doctor fish, and we'll gnaw all the dead tissue away.

I suppose, her mother said then, holding the cutting board with the cake's remnants over the garbage can as if it were a ceremonial platter, I will just have to start again.

4

David didn't know what brought the memory back. Perhaps it was being pushed in there with all the roses, that smell reminding him of the mother's cheap eau de toilette, or the slight panic he was beginning to feel with the garden tour closing in. That run-in with his neighbour hadn't helped, or the girls coming to fill the house again . . . maybe it was all of it combined that had brought the awful memory back.

They'd been fighting all weekend, David and his friend, since the minute they'd left school together on Friday. They were thirteen and it was supposed to be fun, a weekend sleepover on the friend's farm, but they'd fought over everything: who was going to have the last slice of bread and jam, who was going to climb the tree first, who was going to have the biggest pillow and the softest cover and who, on that Sunday morning, was going to wear the old rubber gumboots and who was going to wear the leather boots that laced above the ankle and were warm, because it was late fall and neither child was dressed properly for the cold.

It's my house, the friend said, the trump card he'd been playing all weekend long. I get to choose. I get whatever I want.

But I'm your guest, David protested, drawing his shoulders up and trying to look more powerful. Hating his friend, again, for being so greedy and snivelling and spoiled. For thwarting him at every turn. For lording it over him. For making him feel small and inferior, just because he had a whole farm and David lived in town in a mean house with barely a yard and nothing to do all day but stay inside or walk the streets where a hundred sets of eyes were watching, ready to jump on any hint of vandalism. Where everyone had been swindled by his father's roofing business at least once and would look at David and weigh the benefits of taking him down.

It was raining that morning, and they'd gone to the barn to find something to do until the sun came out and they could go to the river and spend the afternoon chasing fish and making bridges and dams out of anything they could find—logs, cans, tree limbs, whatever was lying around. They'd get up in the hayloft and make a fort, or mess with the horses, or rummage through all the junk in the tack room—whatever they wanted because a kid's life on a farm, David had discovered, was a life without the fun-spoiling oversight of a parent. It was space to roam and the freedom to cut trees with knives and push entire banks into streams to muddy them.

David saw the spider first. It was in the middle of the barn floor, a huge daddy-long-legs frozen there and waiting for them to make the first move. David grabbed a metal pole from the floor and raced to squash it, pole straight up, and brought it down again and again as the spider darted to escape. His friend grabbed the pole as well, trying to wrestle it for himself, wanting all the glory of the kill. Asserting his right to it. And when the pole hit the faulty overhead line and a thousand volts of electricity came coursing through, David's friend got the best of that too. The rubber boots David was wearing bounced the current back, and the leather boots, with his friend inside them, took it all. David had wished the little prick dead and now he was, right in front of him, all his muscles cramped around that pole. Scorch marks at the corners of his mouth, as if his scream had been flames licking at his cheeks.

That scream had stayed with David for a long time. Years. He could hear it now. High pitched and shrill like an animal, all one note, not the keening modulation of the boy's mother prying her son off the rod and falling with him to the barn floor, trying to wake him up, kissing and slapping his face . . . her sounds the same as David's own, as they'd both sobbed and yelled over the boy's dead body, David seized with guilt—a terrible accident the mother placed squarely on him, and he knew she was right.

Even his parents, he remembered, had asked him why he'd done it. What had possessed him to do such a foolish thing? Hadn't they taught him better than that? And the price, they'd said piously, as if he didn't already know it down to the grubby soles of his feet, was a human life. A *human life*. They didn't need to send him to his room to think about what he'd done because David sent himself, for a week, refusing to come out—pissing out the window and shitting in a drawer. He'd cried more tears in that week than he'd thought possible.

Funny thing about that kid, he'd told his wife once, when she'd brought it up again. The day before, we'd been playing on dirt—a big pile of it in a field—and it slid and buried him. I grabbed a shovel to dig him out and just as I was going to drive it in, the ground shook and it was his face. Right there. Just where I was going to put that shovel in. I would have put it in his face.

It's too bad you didn't, Margaret had said coolly. He would have been at a hospital instead of in that barn. He'd be alive.

David reached for another stake, sucking his hand where he'd snagged it on a thorn, thinking about what she'd said—that he might have helped that boy by hurting him, by staving in his face. That a disfigured life was better than no life at all.

He jammed the stake in. Tied the rose to it. Thinking how much easier it had made it, that she understood. That she took his spikes of violence without complaint. Saw their necessity for a full life; a lived life. A life of honesty.

You're passionate, she'd said in the early days, giving it a name. Making it all okay.

Their own rooms of course, Margaret snapped, as if her daughter's question, "Which rooms should I prepare?" was just another attempt to get at her. To make her feel that she wasn't performing adequately. That it was her job to get the bedrooms ready. But why should it be? What, after all, was the point of raising children if you couldn't lay tasks on them. And she had enough to do already, just trying to make her husband see sense about the garden tour he'd arranged for two days hence.

Cancel it, she'd told him. Unequivocal.

It was the way he'd inclined his head, just slightly, and mumbled his response, that told her he had no intention of cancelling anything. That he didn't see how Pippa and Jax arriving had to make life come to a standstill, and how a luxury coach with fifty-two gawking strangers would be like unleashing locusts. And how she couldn't withstand another plague. Couldn't withstand his inevitable rage when the whole venture crumbled, as she knew that it would.

We, she'd said, steadying herself against the island, are already weakened by the state of things.

But David had seen only her cigarette's ash beginning to quiver as it lengthened, about to fall across the back of her hand, and he'd pictured stubbing it out to give her the stigmata he knew she craved. And the royal "we" was *his* to use, not hers.

Yes, darling, was all he'd said. Slow and measured. *I understand.*

Georgina started with her own room on the second floor, determined to be comfortable if she had to stay there, as her mother said she did. "Your sister's quarantine," she was calling it. Her room was across the landing from her parents' room which, in that house, meant it was twenty leagues across a sea of carpets layered on top of one another. At some point their parents had gone through an extended phase of exotic trips abroad, and more carpets had been sent back than could possibly be accommodated even by all the floors in that enormous house. So there were kilims draped over tables and Kashmir rugs hanging from walls and, in every space free of furniture, piles of rugs cushioning your step like a luxurious patterned turf. It made moving through the house strangely like travelling through an Ottoman court.

Out of control, Georgina thought, pushing in the door to her old room. Avoiding, instinctively, the creak in the threshold. Her father's clothes were draped over the wingback chair and his dressing gown was hanging from one of the bed's columns—her parents' marriage like a faulty switch that often propelled him out of their shared bed and into his daughter's four-poster now that she'd moved out. On the nightstand was a box of tissues and three bottles of pills, and the duvet was pushed back where her father must have left it when he'd risen. He'd never made a bed in his life, she was sure of it.

Georgina sighed.

She paused at the enormous window and looked down at the section of garden she could see outside the front door, sitting for a moment on the window seat to take it in. To calm herself with the careful geometry of the circle and its plantings and its regimented style of gravel pathways like some Celtic knot or simple mandala. Already, being back in her childhood home was wearing on her. Her mother was right: a tour group was a bad idea with both Jax and Pippa arriving that night. They'd all be trapped in the house until the tour was over, and Georgina knew, from other tours her mother had hosted multiple times a year, that the people pressing the flower beds underneath the ground-floor windows wouldn't be able to resist lifting their eyes and peering in to see what further glories were contained inside that great house set in the midst of the sculpted landscape. These tours, she knew, weren't really for gardeners at all. Those fanatics were busy tilling their own soil, coaxing life, pruning madly to force a second bloom. No, these tours were filled with lifestyle tourists who wanted to pretend, for one afternoon, that they were to the manor born.

As if, Georgina thought, pulling the sheets back from the double bed, that's a benefit. An achievement the world could agree upon.

She bundled the two large sheets together and left the room, passing through the sewing room with its wall of cupboards stuffed full of sheet sets, pillowcases, draperies, lace tablecloths and stacks and stacks of textiles that had accumulated there over the years. The ironing board was set up in one corner with its iron and spray bottle of starch, as if one still dressed formally for dinner. Or for anything. Georgina herself was still in the T-shirt and shorts that she'd slept in. And they weren't even hers. Just something she'd pulled from her husband's dresser the night before because all of her own were dirty, and she'd just wanted to get into bed and go to sleep and get the whole thing started at her parents'. Get it over with.

You're so money, a girlfriend had told her once. You can wear rags because your house is so obviously a fucking mansion.

The back hall, which the sewing room let into, was narrow and plain because it was the servants' wing. Two bedrooms opened off it, one of them Pippa's, and they were so small in relation to the windows the house was studded with that they seemed all glass, and were bright and sunny and gave the impression of conservatories An unexpected grandeur for a servant—as if the architect had understood oppression and the need for stolen spaces that opened out to a horizon wider than you could ever imagine for yourself. There was just enough wall space for a bed and a tiny nightstand but nothing else, so their parents had paid a carpenter to build drawers into those bedrooms' closets for their girls to have somewhere to put their clothes. That was one thing Georgina would admit about her parents: they'd always been good at compartments. At relegating and dividing, even if they didn't always get it right.

At the far end of the hallway, at the foot of the stairs leading to the third floor, was a large closet with a porcelain utility sink and a jumble of mops and brooms and dusters. The second-floor vacuum cleaner was in there too, and as Georgina opened the laundry chute to toss the dirty sheets down, she glanced at the closet and wondered if she should vacuum as well. Thinking that she may as well make herself useful. Thinking that it was just like Pip to drop her bomb when it would inflict the most damage, inconveniencing everyone. Pippa never considered anyone else but herself. Georgina's husband had just looked at her when she'd told him she was moving back in with her parents for as long as it took to straighten Pippa out. Days, weeks, she didn't know. They were both academics and on summer break from their classes, and with only one child between them to manage, all he could do was nod. Their professional lives bled effortlessly into their personal ones, and if he were to challenge her it would first have to be researched, stated clearly and peer reviewed, and neither of them had the time, or desire, for that. Their life together operated under the mandate of least resistance. There'd been a time, at the very beginning, when they'd tried risk—even sex in the campus library's stacks late at night—but neither had taken to it, and they'd quickly settled into a life of studied repetition and maturity. If Georgina said her family needed her, it wouldn't even occur to her husband to question it. Or for Georgina not to go.

35

She yanked the vacuum cleaner from the closet and its cord spilled out all over the floorboards, because whoever had used it last had just dumped it in the closet without spooling the cord properly. Doors in this house, Georgina thought, are always shut tight against mess. Thankful, again, that the home she'd made with her husband was the opposite of that, with everything new and in its place so that day-to-day tasks could be accomplished without having to wrestle them. All it took—she stooped to gather the cord up—was a system. And the will to follow it.

She plugged the vacuum in without even having to think about where the outlet was, her old bedroom's geography so deeply imbedded in her, and the machine started up immediately. The power switch was broken. The third-floor vacuum, she thought, would be even worse. Items in that house always seemed to degrade the higher up they got and the entire third floor, with its three huge bedrooms and two hallways and bathroom and storage closets, was a repository for things deemed too damaged to be shown. It was the shut-away space. Jax's bedroom was up there which seemed, Georgina sneered, about right. Thinking they should probably stick Pippa up there too.

Prenatal depression, their mother had said. The diagnosis Pippa was flying home on. It was easy for Georgina to imagine how it had gone—her little sister crying over the phone and their mother taking the bait—because Pippa had always been good at that. At manipulation. At getting everyone to do what she wanted them to do. And even though she'd made a life and family for herself in New Zealand, a place Georgina only knew by its lack of anything other than indigenous art, here she still was, making them all jump. Georgina supposed that she had to give her father some points for not having fallen so completely for Pippa's drama that he'd cancelled the tour. He might have agreed to pay for the flight (how could he not?), but what other concessions had he made? Knowing her father, Georgina suspected the answer was none. Pushing the vacuum head into the corners, she knew she had to give him credit for that. For staying the course. For being, like this house, a well-reasoned edifice—a facade that she liked to think she projected herself. A way in which they were alike.

How'd she get them to let her fly? Georgina had asked her mother.

Them?

The airline, her doctor . . .

Oh, you know how well she carries her pregnancies. She didn't tell them.

But, isn't that dangerous?

Their mother had simply flicked a hand at the suggestion that danger, in this case, was even a consideration. Don't be silly, was all she'd said.

5

Margaret watched her eldest daughter's car vanish down the driveway, off to the supermarket to stock the house with food.

That is what's so good about Georgina. She never has to be told. All I have to do, Margaret thought, is hint and that's always enough.

The house was empty now, just herself inside, David still out in the garden, and so she turned and climbed the back stairs as automatically as you might lift a bowl from the sink and place it in the dishwasher rack. These were the times when she worked. When she hid herself away, in that room over the kitchen where no one would ever look for her, to assemble her collages. She'd always worked on them in bits and pieces, in stolen moments like this that wouldn't raise suspicions about where she was or what she was doing. About why she was unavailable. Sometimes the work went quickly and she finished entire sheets at once but sometimes, like now, she would stand in the middle of all the accumulated material and not know where to start. She'd put a sheet of paper on the desk or at her feet and just look at it, trying to let some sort of impulse take over because this was a compulsion she couldn't control and even after all this time, years and years and years, she hadn't discovered a way to trigger it.

She heard someone cross the drive just then—her husband, probably—and that was all it took. Her hands began picking things up and laying them down, and at her feet the blank sheet of paper began to fill with an urgency that was so focused anyone would be forgiven for assuming that Margaret was following a plan. Was adhering to a set of instructions she'd picked from a rotating carousel for an activity whose end result was meant to decorate your home. But as she worked, the chaos of what she was making became evident, because what emerged was not a balanced composition to hang above a couch, or a flutter of whimsy to brighten a powder room, or simple colourful shapes for a nursery . . . her canvas was becoming a base for towering stacks of debris that Margaret was overlapping like core samples from a landfill, as if the back side of the paper had been punched and extruded upwards to reveal what it was covering— all those levels of habitation going right down to the limestone that the house was set upon.

Margaret worked without pause, feeling she needed to finish before everyone was back because their arrivals would only signal the beginning of another layer and an entirely new piece she would have to construct. The whole family, back in that house again, was an event she'd have to put down.

—

After they'd married, Margaret had continued to paint. David had his residency and she'd had her art classes, and none of that changed. They moved into an apartment, bought a new bed and some mismatched furniture, and since Margaret was still enrolled in classes it was obvious that she would keep painting. That she'd need a few shelves in the kitchen to store her supplies on, and a corner of the living room for an easel because now, with a husband, they both agreed that she shouldn't have to work in the department's studios all the time. David liked it, he told her, when she worked at home. *It helps me to understand how beauty's made*, he charmed. And she complied because she was still awed by his pronouncements and still believed they pulled her into a discourse she'd been waiting for all her life. He liked to watch her working, and her canvases, as if to make it easier for him to see from his seat across the room, became progressively larger until she was painting entire cityscapes against backgrounds of hills and vales. When he talked about the Elizabethans and their prodigy houses, her cities became sprawling estates and the hills became walled pleasure gardens full of carnations. When he instructed her on the Edwardians, she started painting hermitages on the shores of man-made lakes and flagstone paths disappearing into the woods as if she'd come to it on her own. A natural overflow of all the ideas they shared. Already, their sex life was so perfectly tuned that it seemed right that their day-to-day would be similarly paired. That they would be the same in everything, reflect one another— her art mirroring his mind. He was rough when he touched her, and she invited that because it was something novel only they could have. On his side, no one else had ever submitted so willingly, and on hers, no one else had ever tried. It had a shock that made their dull surroundings seem more glorious than they were and it gave them, both of them, a claim to something raw. He rarely left a mark on her and even when he did it was always somewhere concealed, just for the two of them. An echo of the boldness and originality they thought they shared and needed.

When they moved to Hamilton after David qualified, things began to change. And when they bought the house overlooking the city, Margaret knew then that it was finished. Her painting, which had trickled along at their first house when the girls were small, stopped completely at this new house because how could she compete with what was all around her? With that gorgeous complex canvas below the cliff? And so instead, that first winter when the ground was frozen three feet down and the garden dormant, the collages had started. And this time, Margaret knew not to clear a shelf or use a corner of the living room. The serious work of her creations, in that private room upstairs—she knew to keep them to herself. To use what was at hand, to work with texture and volume because those were the things most lacking, and exactly what she would have to provide for herself. In the summers there was the garden—but in the winters there was nothing but the family stuck inside the house. And her husband had surpassed her in fearlessness. His touch, still rough, was now more often inclined to cruelty—and her role had become equilibrium. To keep everything—the family, the household—together and functioning. And to do that, sometimes she had to lock herself away.

—

Georgina filled the refrigerator and cupboards with food as if laying in provisions for the long haul. There were tins and tins of stew and tuna fish, heads of lettuce, bags of vegetables, every kind of meat, cheeses, breads, chips and crackers, gnocchi, tomato sauce, capers and olives. Coffee, tea, milk, cream, butter . . . the shelves, she thought as she put the groceries away, a replica of the store itself. More than enough to scratch meals from, to feed everybody, a chore she knew would fall to her because the others looked to her to keep the household running. She was firstborn. Even now it was expected of her, and she was nothing if not dutiful.

She spent the rest of the afternoon cooking and tidying, sorting through the Tupperware, throwing out mouldy crusts of bread and organizing all the roasting pans and baking sheets. Filling the kitchen with enough noise that her parents, for the most part, stayed away. Her father came to the house to have his lunch but ate it on the porch because, he told her—making a great show of it—he was too dirty to come inside, and it wasn't worth cleaning himself up because there were still *acres* that needed tending to. He lingered in the doorway until Georgina, turning from the open cupboard she was sorting through, asked if he needed any help.

Tomorrow, he said, pleased that she hadn't forgotten what was most important. Tomorrow I'll put you to work.

Her mother drifted in and out, putting the currants and raisins and apricots on to boil and sifting the dry ingredients, easing past Georgina to get the eggs—stretching the making of another cake so that she could impede every task Georgina had set for herself just as she was completing them. Margaret's timing honed to remind this daughter whose kitchen this still was.

42

Early dinner tonight, Margaret said, sliding the cake into the oven and setting the timer. Nothing fancy. You know your father will eat anything.

Georgina made too much food on purpose so there'd be leftovers for her sisters to reheat when they arrived. Already planning. Already beginning to devise systems to make the whole venture more efficient. Two chickens roasted whole with gravy and potatoes, nothing special, but the way her father crowed over the one she brought to the table, anyone would think they were suckling pigs turned manually on a spit. Commenting, with every downward slice of the carving knife, how succulent and perfectly cooked it was. Skewering the potatoes with his matching bone-handled fork and noting their crisped skins and soft insides; ladling minted peas and parsnips and carrots onto each plate with the flourish of someone doling out treats.

Yes, he said triumphantly, looking down at his plate. This is a fine meal after a day's hard labour. He looked at his wife and his daughter, feeling generous, wanting them to share his pleasure because even they had to admit that this was something to celebrate. That there were such good things on the way. And Georgina, even though she knew there was a second meaning to his comments—that his praise was an indictment of the meals his wife cooked for him—couldn't help feeling appreciated and rewarded for her efforts. Thankful that her father, at least, had recognized her value.

Margaret bided her time. She waited until he went for seconds of the gravy and meat, and then she asked about the garden tour, how the organizers had reacted to his cancelling, whether they wanted to rebook next summer—surely in June— when the garden is at its best and worth seeing. I expect, she said casually, lining her plate up in the centre of her placemat, that their ticket sales were low anyway. I expect it was a relief to them.

David answered her through a mouth full of potato, deliberately unintelligible. He cut his chicken into small bites and kept feeding himself, swiping each forkful through the congealing gravy, studiously avoiding eye contact with this wife who'd finished her tiny meal and was sitting in her chair, at his right hand, watching this performance of squirming nonchalance. It was obvious the tour was going ahead, that he hadn't cancelled anything. He'd spent the entire day out in the garden tidying and his hands were so cut up that they looked like he'd held them down in a bucket full of rats scratching to get out. His fingernails were black with dirt and he'd left the wheelbarrow in the driveway, ready for tomorrow and all the clipping and pruning he said still needed to be done.

Dad, Georgina asked then, attempting to diffuse things before the yelling started. Wanting to rescue him because she thought her mother was being unfair, her father having worked hard all day. Already so beaten down. Can I use your car to pick Pippa up? In case she has luggage. Mine's so small.

David didn't answer without pausing first, because every one of his girls had wrecked a family car. He still didn't know what he'd done to deserve, or create, such recklessness.

All right, he said like a judge giving his ruling. You did cook an exquisite meal.

Why wouldn't she have luggage? Margaret said, looking from

her husband to her daughter as if they'd missed the essential truth of it. She is coming to stay, after all.

There, thought Margaret to herself. *That* trumps your bloody garden tour.

6

It was hard not to think of high school every time Georgina drove this way. The road leading to the cut down the mountain, which would take her out to the highway and to the airport north of Toronto, went right past the campus. When she got a red light at the top of the hill, as she did now, she had to sit there and stare at it until the light turned green. Stare at the ten acres of athletic fields rimmed with clipped hedges; a shell of English public school gravitas. Headmaster, prefects, even a dining hall and chapel, as if the windows looked out onto a heath rather than dandelion-laced North American grass that was deep in Canadian snow four months of the year. The pupils all belonged to houses named after Scottish rivers that translated, Georgina had always thought, into something too grasping and desperate to be proud of: Earn, Ore, More, Tilt. This, after all, was the place where she'd been taught that art was something you did for fun. Relaxation. Art *therapy*. Highfield-Strathclyde College was an incubator for doctors and lawyers, fundraisers and philanthropists, captains of industry—for young adults to become fully formed productive members of society, not pariahs who bled the system dry. Because art, she'd learned, wasn't worth a second look unless it was sanctified by history.

Georgina braked before accelerating into another curve in the road down the escarpment. The idea that she should make art had never even been held out as a possibility. It wasn't something you built an adult life around. It was, her teachers had told her when she pressed them, a selfish act. The sort of choice someone from a lesser school might make; someone without her advantages and opportunities. Someone out to waste her life. Highfield-Strathclyde had preached the responsibility of the few to the many but not, Georgina had only come to realize as she got older, in a democratic sense. Not to *give* power away, but to *keep* it. Not to take your riches and divide them among the poor, but to keep accruing them so that the bastion of a higher society would endure. Because, their model taught with its prefects, house captains, head boy and head girl, the world must have its shining examples of success. Its hierarchy of wealth.

And art? Architecture, perhaps, but not art. And especially not today, when the word was attached to superficial acts of expression that were dumped on an audience without any provenance of thought. Colourful vomit on a canvas—just because. A silent vigil in a gallery—why not. A tangle of cotton in a corner like lint in a giant's laundry room—*ironic*. Instead, Georgina had placed herself right in the solid centre of verifiable masters—Van Gogh, Matisse, Picasso, Derain—like a custodian.

And yet . . . she had an invitation, there in her purse, to a former graduate student's opening at a gallery downtown. Somehow, Georgina thought, that young woman had managed it—to enter the academy, but then to step away and produce her own works and offer them up to be judged. It might not be the Louvre but it was happening now, and Georgina couldn't help feeling that there was something to that—something she'd missed. Something she hadn't been brave enough to try. Maybe . . . maybe it wasn't too late.

If she could see past the forested greenway on her left to the western edge of the city, Georgina would see the university she'd spent her entire career at—from undergraduate to associate professor—with only one fleeting year spent in Museum Studies at the University of Leicester, where she'd taken classes in buildings that were enlarged versions of the house she'd grown up in. It had been her only extended time away from Hamilton, and sometimes she found herself looking at that line on her vitae and trying to remember what it had felt like, living somewhere else. There were isolated memories, corroborated by the few photographs she had of that year, but even they were becoming unreliable and the whole experiment in living abroad—which her father had championed and bankrolled only because it was Mother Britain—was fading away, and her entire life seemed wrapped by this town and the house that presided over it. More so, even, than the house she shared with her husband and their son, which felt somehow *provisional*. A sort of camp.

The black maples and sumac and birch on either side of the narrow road taking her down the escarpment had the weary August appearance of leaves that have taken on too much. Too much wind and rain and heat and pollution, and their stems, if she could stop and get out and look, would be thinned and getting ready to drop. Some of the trees, in the valleys where the sun only peeked, were already turning. Summer, Georgina realized, was almost over. And what had she accomplished?

The house was quiet, now that Georgina was gone. Despite its size, it registered even the slightest absence. David and Margaret were seated together on the porch, as was their custom after supper, so silent that the receding crunch of the car's tires on the gravel still hung in the air twenty minutes later. Margaret was smoking and looking out over the city, the day's heat still laid across it like a fallen cloud, and David was reading through the newspaper that had been sitting there since morning. His absorption a rebuke—*I have been waiting to read this all day . . .* and *Look at me, just a labourer, but hungry for self-improvement.* The paper was warped and buckled by the humidity, and already yellowing, but he was looking at it anyway. Another instance, his posture said, of how the entire world undervalues me.

Neither of them could summon the desire to speak. Not because there weren't any new outrages to vocalize, because certainly there were, but because of all the old injuries whose cruelties were so great that they lay, always, just beneath whatever passed between them. And at times like this, they knew from experience, those grievances would overwhelm if given half a chance and neither of them could afford that because each had their hobby horse to ride, and neither wanted to surrender the lead—because each felt they had the upper hand. Margaret had orchestrated the rescue of their daughter, and David had created a public showcase for his acumen.

Did you get enough? she said finally, pushing the words through her teeth.

Darling?

Dinner. Did you get enough?

David lowered the paper to his lap and turned, in the sulphurous light cast by the driveway's single floodlight, to face this wife backlit by the city, her cigarette throbbing.

Yes. Thank you. Georgina did a very nice job.

Yes. She did.

And David knew that his wife's seemingly casual affirmation was in fact freighted with the contention that if their daughter had done well, it was only because of the lifelong work she'd invested in her. And in all of them.

Philippa, he countered, laying Margaret's failure on the floor between them.

And there it was. The initial cut. The familiar edge he'd rub against her until she begged him for more.

That tour, she answered, drawing the last syllable out so it floated across and brushed his cheek like a kiss. Like her lips against his neck, taunting him to go back at her, a little deeper each time, both of them thrumming now, because this also was a custom of theirs—sniping at each other until the words reached their climax and became physical.

7

Pippa was, to Georgina, barely recognizable when the customs doors slid open and she came through them. There was the pregnancy, of course, but it was more than that. It was as if her actions and thoughts were slowed down to the tempo of something as primordial as one revolution of the sun and the moon. She seemed tidal. In motion, but deceptively so. You'd have to close your eyes for an hour and reopen them to notice a change, and even then it would be so slight you wouldn't be sure it was true. Georgina had thought this emergency flight home was nothing but impulse and drama—both states she knew Pippa thrived on—but now, Georgina thought this crisis might actually be real. Not just something else Pippa had invented for herself.

When Georgina, shepherding her through arrivals and out to the car, asked Pippa where her bags were, she only twitched the shoulder her backpack hung from. One of her kids' bags, Georgina thought, looking at its zipper jangling with novelty key chains.

This is it? No suitcase?

She pushed Pippa ahead of her through the revolving door and out to the covered roadway where passengers were queuing for taxis or hotel shuttles, thankful for the noise and commotion which made it impossible to talk. Because Georgina didn't know what to say to her little sister without betraying how shocked she was. Georgina, trained to analyze, had already summarized Pippa and reduced her down to an archetype: vagabond.

Pippa stopped just then and looked down at her right foot, which had come forward without its black rubber sandal. It lay behind her, upside down, its thong snapped. After looking at it for a few seconds, she just continued on without it.

Your—. Georgina jogged back to retrieve the shoe and catch up to Pippa, who'd stopped now. Enough awareness, at least, to realize she didn't know where the car was parked. And likely, Georgina thought, didn't even know what it looked like. It had been three or four years since Pippa had last been over, and her father's car had only been purchased a few years ago. A replacement after the last accident.

We're over here, Georgina said, transferring the bag from her sister's shoulder to her own, stuffing the broken flip-flop into the mesh pocket on the side as Pippa trudged along just behind her, not seeming to mind her foot against the oil-stained concrete of the parking garage. Not seeming to mind anything. Just following, mutely, and settling into the car as though she might go to sleep, her whole body pressed into the seat like she was custom made for it. Perfectly content to take whatever form was presented to her.

I thought you'd have luggage, Georgina said as they crept down the spiralling exit ramp. Mum said you'd have luggage, so I brought Dad's car because it's bigger. For the luggage. Repeating herself, trying to fill the emptiness and not comment on her sister's smell, which was filling the car now with the sweet thickness of filth. Of sweat and dirt in layers that must have accumulated over days and days, because this was more than just an eighteen-hour flight. This was a prolonged neglect. A determined savagery.

Georgina kept her window down after paying at the kiosk.

Are you hungry? she asked, slowing down at the traffic light before turning onto the road out to the highway. I made chicken, she said, trying not to retch at the thought of eating. A roast. But we could stop for something now if you want.

Pippa didn't answer. Just sat there until Georgina asked again, looking right at her, and then she shook her head, shifting her hands on her lap around the enormous mound of her stomach. "Prenatal depression" their mother had said, emphasizing the "pre" in a tone that had seemed, to Georgina, coloured with disbelief. As if what she was really saying was, "Well, that's what Pippa wants us to think." Even though Pippa's husband had told her that their doctor had prescribed an antidepressant, their mother always liked to present herself as closer to the truth than anyone else.

Perhaps, thought Georgina, that's what I'm seeing—the effect of that. A semi-conscious medicated state.

She merged onto the busy highway to begin their journey back home, trying not to stare at Toronto gleaming to the east in the sun's falling light. The air screaming through the open window. She didn't need to be reminded that her entire life had been spent on the margins, and that she'd never had the courage to be anywhere else. Georgina concentrated on the traffic signs because it had been a while since she'd picked someone up at the airport and if she wasn't vigilant, she'd end up downtown in the big city on a Thursday night instead of on her way back to Hamilton. And this, she thought, is not how I've envisioned entering it. Nothing triumphal about arriving in my parents' car with a damaged little sister in the passenger seat. Her arrival in Toronto, she'd always dreamt, would be heralded by miracles. A full choir of angels with trumpets, wings beating the air like an invasion of butterflies. Not limping in, all broken, like this.

By the time they entered the heavily wooded lane, the sun was almost down and the distance had been stretched by the shadows. It had been a long day and it seemed to take an age to get to the gateway and enter the drive, but then it was there—the house—in front of a purpling sky, timeless and magnificent. Even Pippa sensed the change and sat forward. Georgina slowed the car, hardly rolling now. She noted each light that was on—the kitchen, the family room, her bathroom, an upstairs hallway, and the porch light where she knew her mother would be reclining and watching their progress toward the house. Waiting, on tenterhooks, for her youngest daughter to come home. Ready to pounce. Their father would already be in bed.

Once they were parked, Pippa stayed where she was until Georgina came around and opened her door, and then she got out and walked mechanically to the porch steps and to her mother who was waiting there, in the yellow of the bug light, willing her daughter to keep moving until she was safe.

After tomorrow, Georgina wanted to shout, a tour's coming but we'll be all right. We just have to stay inside until they're gone.

But Pippa wouldn't have heard her anyway. Their mother had her now, smoothing her hair back, running a hand over the coming grandchild, adjusting Pippa's cardigan so it sat perfectly on her thin shoulders and marvelling, in a loud voice, at how absolutely terrible she looked. She'd never seen, she howled, a more destitute-looking young woman in all her life. Looking around for someone, anyone, to agree with her. But Georgina was lingering at the car, waiting for the initial shock waves to subside, the thinnest sliver of a respite before re-entering the fray.

I'll get Pip some dinner, Georgina said when she mounted the porch, going inside and leaving the two of them out there alone. She was glad to have someone else to shoulder the burden of home for a while. Something else for her mother to focus on.

And there isn't, she said as the screen door snapped shut behind her, any luggage. Unable to resist.

When Jax's taxi drove up to the house at one in the morning, only the light over the kitchen stove was on. No one had waited up for her, not even her mother, but Jax had expected that. Of the three sisters, she was the one who always escaped notice—and that was how she liked it. Even now, when there was nothing to hide—no alcohol or drugs or boyfriend's mouth leaving marks on her—it was better to just walk inside without being confronted. Without someone—their mother—trying to figure

you out. Jax was the middle child but she'd spent her life inhab-
iting that place in the lineage as if she were the forgotten end.

They were all there now, the house was full. It shifted around
them as they slept, little creaks and groans, readjusting all the
heartbeats until they were synchronized, because in all things, it
demanded symmetry. If one left, another stayed; if one was
born, another might have to die.

Friday

8

I'll look in on her, David called out from the bathroom. On my way downstairs.

Philippa's already down there, his wife answered weakly from the adjoining bedroom, and David knew that she was curled up on her side, the arm under her head flung straight out like a boom across his pillow. She's throwing up, his wife said. In the bathroom. Downstairs.

Oh, he said. As though it's my fault, he thought. As though I am to blame for wanting to try again for a son. For insisting on one more go at it. For wearing you down. For being—he looked in the mirror—an animal. He placed a scrap of toilet paper on the tiny cut along his jaw. *Leopard*, he thought, baring his fangs.

Do you need anything, darling? he asked wearily, knowing he'd get only an exhalation. Not a word, but just as expressive as a no. She might sleep all morning. He didn't think Margaret had slept more than an hour in bits and pieces since Pippa phoned and now that Pippa was here, it would be his wife's pattern to bottom out. At least it might keep her out of the way. He still had work to do if tomorrow was to be a triumph, and he wouldn't have her ruining it.

She listened to him fiddling about in the bathroom, taking his time, so plodding and deliberate it made her want to scream. She raised her arm and dropped it like a hammer on his pillow.

You could turn the air conditioning on, she called out. It's stuffy in here.

Darling?

The air conditioning. It's hot.

He was standing in the doorway looking down at her. She could sense him there, his controlled breathing, and she knew he was thinking that the air conditioning would come on when it was supposed to, that it was pre-set, and interfering would throw the whole system off.

Hot? In here?

She twisted her head back over her shoulder in the direction of his silhouette, squinting against the bright morning sunshine. Yes. It is hot. In here. Channelling enough provocation and hurt into her voice to warn him there was plenty more where that came from. An entire storehouse. Forty-seven years of it, in fact.

You have your covers on, he said just above a whisper.

She flicked her head back, cinched the duvet around her shoulders and dropped the hammer arm again, repeatedly. He would turn it on, she knew. Just enough to say he'd done it, enough that she couldn't blame him for not listening, but not enough it would run and cool the room properly.

—

David trod down the steps, remembering, when he saw the bath-room door shut on the ground floor, what his wife had said about Pippa and thinking that he should have gone down the back stairs instead because sickness unnerved him. He might be a doctor, but only of skin—not what was down inside. Not what was always—he shuddered—trying to rise up and make us see what we're really made of, which is messy, pungent and raw. And wasn't that precisely why the girls were here? To deal with that? He adjusted the thermostat a few degrees lower, resolving not to think about it again until afternoon, and then he'd put it back to where it was supposed to be. If my wife kept normal hours, he thought, none of this would be necessary. I could just get on with things.

He caught sight of himself in the hall's floor-length mirror—and wasn't that the very picture of success? He stopped to appraise himself. That compact man of average height whose hair was only greying at the temples and still bounced when he walked because it was still a full head of hair—almost embarrass-ing at his age, how much hair he still had. He ran a hand through it. He imagined the girls at the office whispering about it being a weave or a transplant or, at the very least, an exquisite dye-job and he expected, any day now, that they'd sidle up and ask him where he'd had the work done so they could book their hus-bands in. Make them young and virile and interesting, those sad-sack men who slowed their cars at the curb just enough so their wives could jump in. A technique, he imagined, they'd perfected cruising prostitutes. Years since they'd handled their wives. And I handled mine, he thought complacently, only last night.

Tomorrow, he thought grandly, is the garden tour. Breakfast first, and then I will dress and get started. He'd not let his wife, with her invented crises, spoil things this time.

The tea bags were nearly finished and someone, he saw as he reached for it, had used the sugar spoon to stir, putting it back in the sugar bowl afterwards so now the measuring end was caked with dirty crystals. It was small things like this that smacked of laziness and infuriated him. He knew it would have been his wife at midnight or one a.m. just drifting through the house making messes, and no thought of who'd have to put up with them. The entire counter, if he looked, would be full of similar violations, but he knew from long experience just to concentrate on the simple tasks of porridge and tea and then get out. He was the only man in a clutch of women and he had to look out for himself because they were always trying to turn him, and he'd be buggered if he'd let them do it. They can keep their irrational messes, he thought, for themselves. A trap he'd avoid. A stumble he refused to take. Just another instance, he thought, of being better—*veni vidi vici*—than everyone.

The porch door swung out and Jax came in.

Hola, she said brightly, her bursting good health like a slap.

Jacqueline, her father answered, his hand paused at the kettle. I didn't expect to see you up this early.

Jax grinned, lifting her foot to show him her running shoes. I jog every morning now. Three miles.

You jog, David repeated vaguely, crossing the kitchen to give his daughter a welcome. For exercise?

Well, yeah.

Good flight? he asked.

Jax shrugged. Good enough.

Sleep well?

Great. That room's like a crypt, it's so quiet.

David nodded, returning to the kettle.

What does that make my room, I wonder. A sub-crypt? *Crypta sub locus*. Tea, darling?

No, thanks. I haven't gone running yet. Was just stretching and heard someone in here, so thought I'd say hi. Thought it might be Pippa.

Pippa? No. And your mother's in bed. Georgie's up there somewhere too.

Just us early birds, then. Jax laughed. Bet you never thought you'd hear me say that.

David smiled, as if those awful teenage years of hers were a fond memory they shared.

You know, he said, nursing his tea, I could use some help in the garden today. Since you're here, and awake.

Sure. At the usual rate?

David looked momentarily thrown.

Don't you remember? You used to pay us five dollars an hour. Subject, of course, to whether we did a good job or not.

Did I?

Yeah. You'd go around at the end of the day and evaluate what we'd done and then pay out accordingly. Quality control, you called it.

Well. I was teaching you to do work you could stand behind.

And saving yourself some money, Jax joked.

But her father bristled, drawing his shoulders back in that gesture Jax recognized as the preamble to an attack.

I'm sure I deserved it, she said quickly. And I can definitely help out today. For free, she grinned, going out and letting the door slam behind her and becoming just a bounding figure framed by the window, leaving David alone in the kitchen with his tea. Needing a minute to reorient himself to this new, and unpleasant, reality of the children back home again. Needing to find a way to make it advantageous.

He retreated, before Pippa the injured or anyone else could come out and delay him, to the other end of the house where he'd laid the accounts out on the enormous walnut table to organize. Where he'd be surrounded by antiques jumbled on credenzas and end tables and mantel and windowsills and stuffed, cheek to jowl, into the glass-fronted sideboard. A lifetime of acquisitions— passing fancies for Waterford and Royal Doulton and Fabergé, anything with a name that would draw a gasp in conversation. A storehouse, he thought complacently as he put his tea down and retied his dressing gown, of my astuteness.

He liked to start his day here, among his possessions, reassuring himself of his success.

Taking his seat at the head of the big table they used only for special occasions, David thought, as he did every time he sank into them, how absolutely correct he'd been to have the chairs reupholstered in padded red velvet. His wife had wanted to keep the chairs in the original leather but he'd gone ahead and had it done, and weeks had passed before she'd even noticed. There was so much, he sighed, that woman doesn't see. So much she didn't give him credit for. She liked to remind him that she suffered, as if he was the cause of that, when really everything he did was for her comfort. He only gave her what he knew she needed.

Over the past week, David had been going through the gardening expenses, and the view of the extravagant herbaceous border outside the window was reassuring. He could have bought a summer cottage with all that money, and furnished it and had a boat or two and taken months off every year to use them with the family, but instead he'd built a garden, maintaining and improving it, flower beds devouring the grass and enough trees felled that they'd kept their fireplaces blazing for the last twenty-seven winters without having to buy any wood. Something to be said for that. Self-sufficiency. It was an investment, he chuckled, that would just keep growing. Would *burn* with returns. Smoke *and* fire. A *bonfire* of earnings.

Something about being there made him giddy. His wife immobile in the room above him while he sat there, his loot spread out. Arley Hall, Beth Chatto, Kew, Castle Howard, Hidcote, Stowe . . . every famous garden they'd ever toured, it was all around him. He'd reproduced the best of each of them right outside, on his own property. A smaller scale perhaps but there is perfection, he mused, in miniatures. If anything, it takes even more skill to get it right—the tiny parterre, the shrunken maze, the child-sized folly, the delicate tracery of a water feature. David likened himself to a duke who'd made a pile of money that would become, with his eventual passing, Old Money, which could be used to maintain The Estate. It was the twenty-first century; a girl could inherit that. Even the Queen had changed the rules of succession to account for a girl. And tomorrow, he was going to show it all off. His private pleasure would become a public park, just long enough for jealousy to overtake his visitors. Because David needed that. And maybe, he dared hope, one of them would go home and take a spade to his own yard and make something lasting and close to beautiful. David had always felt he had a duty to lead by example and thereby force improvements in others who needed them, but didn't have the audacity and vigour (as he did) to undertake them on their own.

He checked his watch. He still had to speak to his wife about the refreshments; to put her to work. The terrace, he thought, shifting his ledgers around, would be the obvious place to serve them. Another hour and he'd turn her out of bed and get her cracking on that. Thinking how reasonable that was, to let her have a little sleep even though her efforts during the night had been small. His orgasm, if he thought about it, had had very little to do with her. And when Jacqueline was back from her exercising, he'd put her to work weeding around the bases of the topiary. Even she, he thought, won't be able to mess that up.

And the others—well, the others would have to wait.

Georgina sat at the big table in the bay window having breakfast by herself. The newspaper, a half-eaten bagel, a cup of coffee and silence. Trying for silence, but it was impossible to escape the fact of Pippa in the room above her. Impossible not to feel the weight of her condition pressing down. A distant sail flashed in the sunshine and it made Georgina think of placards, gleaming white, proclaiming something (Darfur? Free Tibet? Afghanistan?), and of being pulled along by Pippa as she plunged into a demonstration to find her group of activists because *this*—she'd shouted back to Georgina, glowing—is *national*. Not some lame local *bullshit*. It seemed enormous, that crowd, once they were pushing through it. Georgina had grabbed her sister's hand, worried they'd be separated and she'd be left there with no one and no understanding of the cause, and that the zealots would sniff her out. Feed on her apathy, her lack of politics. But as they went deeper and met up with the other local agitators, Georgina became worried for her sister who was like fresh meat, surrounded by all those lions. And not the proud lions of fable, but beasts whose scabbed shanks knocked together and whose backs and shoulders were unequal to the size of their heads. Heads that swivelled at Pippa the moment she arrived; eyes that were feverish, ravenous.

Pippa's "causes" in high school were so changeable that Georgina, a few years into university by then, had briefly assumed the role of mentor to try to straighten her out. Teach her to focus. Get her to identify, at the very least, with a single group because the randomness of her attachments had become—to Georgina, who was still living at home—like a meta-commentary on Georgina's growing sense that she herself was too single-minded and narrow in her choices. Each time Pippa picked a new banner to get behind, it felt like a jab at the constancy of Georgina's path. Like a broadsword to her feet.

Georgina's gaze wandered to the west end of the city, and she thought about her colleague who'd died the week before. Such a stupid death. Gridlocked in a traffic jam on his way to the airport, he'd stepped out to take a piss. He was forty-four, never married, no children, and his mother was driving. He'd climbed over the low wall of the overpass they were stalled on, lost his footing, and fell dick out onto the freeway below. The mother told the faculty everything, an outpouring of information in a long email prompted by guilt because she didn't get out to look for him right away. And what would *you* have done, her mail asked between its lines. Would you have followed him? Would you have told him to stop being a fool and wait for a proper toilet? Blaming herself but, in her tone, also blaming them. As if they were all complicit in the sad state of his life. Within the week, an adjunct claimed his office and his mailbox, and it had started Georgina wondering if she could do it as well. Disappear. Actually put into action her desire to be more than what she was. Because no one, it seemed, would care. She pushed her mug around, imagining her whole life like a parade of oiled soldiers marching over the cliff and drowning themselves in the lake. There must be a way to speed that up, a way to get it done so things can start over again. Somehow go back and take a different path.

Her reveries were interrupted by her sister running past the windows, hopping awkwardly as she pried her shoes off, and diving into the shallow end. Jax had always made a habit of that, just to flout the safety rules and irritate their parents.

So, Georgina thought, she's arrived.

She went to the window and stood there a full five minutes before she was noticed, and then Jax's answer to her wave was a cheeky bottoms-up and water kicked so hard and high it almost wet the glass. Only thing that's changed, Georgina thought as she watched her sister swim, is that she's wearing clothes. A small mercy.

It had probably been a year or more since Jax had been back. More, Georgina decided, remembering that the previous summer Jax and her husband and kids had gone to California instead. Yosemite? San Francisco? Something, anyway, more important than bringing her kids here to spend time with their only Canadian cousin. But Jax has always been like that, Georgina thought, watching her floating on her back with her eyes closed and arms outstretched like an ad for a luxury retreat. Serene. Self-satisfied. Selfish. She's not going to be any help. Why had their mother flown her home, and why had Jax gone along with it?

Turning away, leaving her sister to her pleasure games, Georgina went upstairs to check on Pippa. She found her lying on her side facing the wall, the bedspread half-heartedly dragged over one leg and a hip. Not even dressed, just a towel tucked under her arms. Probably from her shower the night before.

Pips?

Georgina waited a minute.

Philippa, she said again, a little louder, stepping into the room and around the bed, stooping to get a better look—doing what she'd done with her son when he was a baby, creeping in to check if he'd gone to sleep, her stomach tight, waiting for the sharp gasp that always preceded the wail. She pulled the bedspread over Pippa, up around her chin, purposefully a little rough to try and jostle her awake so they could get to the bottom of whatever had brought her there, interrupting their lives, making them nurses and handlers—as if *they* had the answers to *anything*. As if, as a collective force, they were omnipotent. Her sympathy beginning to fall away as she realized how familiar this was—ministering to Philippa. How even as adults, her little sister played the child and expected them to do what they'd always done—look after her.

Georgina looked at the hunting scene above the bed: the trim landscape, surging hounds, and in the background the hunting party with their red coats and top hats, horses carrying them across hedgerows and idyllic fences on hooves so dainty and perfect that the fox would be lucky to be a part of that—the named star of such an impeccable show. She remembered this painting because the artist had placed the fox in the foreground, this side of a hillock, and given it a smile. A frozen, nervous, jaw-clenching smile like a cartoon which made the whole scene absurd and weirdly exceptional, and she'd loved it for that. For that pointed little snub of every hunting scene ever painted, and every pompous house they'd ever hung in. But looking at it now, she realized that the intention was ferocity, not irony, and that the artist had missed the mark. And she supposed that's why her parents had put it there, on that forgotten wall at the forgotten end of the second floor, pushed to the edges by the gorgeously framed copies of Vermeers, Rembrandts and Caravaggios the rest of the house was hung with. This was an original, yes, but a failure.

Georgina and her sisters had been named for boys—George, Jack and Phillip—but they were, in the end, only girls. And nothing much had ever been expected of them.

9

Jax floated on her back, the loose T-shirt billowing around her, and stared up at the early-morning sky without flinching. It was nothing compared to a Florida sky. She knew her parents and sisters would be complaining about the heat but, she sneered, they don't even know what heat is. This—she swanned both her arms out—is practically cold. *Goosebumps all over my body.*

Gripping the pool's coping with her toes to anchor herself there, Jax let her eyes trace the house from its eaves down to its basement windows. Things were different, of course—there'd been improvements, certainly—but the essence of the place hadn't changed. It was still home. When their parents had bought the house, there'd been a metal structure stacked like an Erector set from the ground up to the roof to support the old TV aerial, a metal grid like an oven rack. It had stayed there even as the gardens had grown, and the swimming pool been put in, and the new outdoor furniture was placed in conversation groupings around the patio and terrace, expensive planters bought to define boundaries—the aerial just an eyesore against the cut stone. But for a few glorious years, until their parents got around to removing it, it had been her exit route. All she'd had to do was crawl twenty feet across the steeply pitched roof from a dormer window in the attic, and then climb her way down the tower to freedom. A run through the garden's shadows to the street and, three blocks over, the bus stop and she was away with no curfew.

Jax sank below the pool water now, remembering. Bars, mostly. Bands. Some house parties, although they weren't always along a bus route. For a few months there'd been the off-books reggae club in a back few rooms above a store in the north end, near the lake. She'd been initiated into it because that's how it was—those stolen nights a sketchy network of introductions by alcoholics and addicts who'd vouch for you because you were young or pretty or money enough, and Jax was all three. Sometimes she'd take the city steps instead of waiting for the bus, dropping a hundred feet down the escarpment to the neighbourhood below, which was what she'd done the night Pippa followed her downtown.

I saw you, Pippa said when Jax, turning, saw her slip from shadow to shadow, trailing her. You went right past my window.

You climbed down it too? Jax had said, furious, scarcely listening when Pippa explained she'd gone out through the kitchen door, their parents too busy arguing to notice. Pippa quailing in front of her sister's anger, but impossible now to go back up through those nighttime woods alone.

That your sister? the taller of two boys said.

She followed me, Jax said coldly, making it clear she hadn't brought Pippa along to this rendezvous. The boy kissed her sloppily on the mouth, loosening her up, making her care about nothing else.

Right on, his friend grinned, slinging an arm around Pippa's shoulders like they were together. Come on, little sis. Call me Lucifer. He winked. Luce for short.

Because these two older boys from twelfth grade were relying on Jax to get them into her genuine underground club that was choked—they were counting on it—with weed and sex. It might be a *reggae* club but it was their wet dream rock and roll and they'd been waiting for this for years. Nothing was going to mess that up.

It was a school night—a Wednesday—but that scarcely mattered to the people inside the club. School, for them, was an irrelevance. Most of them were too old even for university. It was like being drawn into a foreign country where a white girl in a bunched-up nightgown might lose herself, and Jax, looking at her sister, laughed: at the clothes she'd thrown on over her pyjamas, at her unease, at what she recognized as arousal. An awakening. The press of sweating bodies in that narrow, high-ceilinged space and the music running through all of them, a collective throbbing . . . what else could they do but give in. It was, Jax would think later, her finest work. The single event she could point to when taking credit for Pippa's subsequent rebelliousness and the absolute genius of how that had taken the attention away from her own exploits, affording her a freedom she wouldn't have had if not for that younger, less careful sister who appeared to be screwing up even more than she was.

Old times, she smiled, coming up for air and feeling suddenly dominant. Just what the doc never orders, but exactly what we always need. Another night out with me will shake Li'l Pips loose of whatever's got hold of her.

After those boys, already two hours past their curfew, had dropped them at the end of the lane, Jax let Pippa take her arm because the lane at night was spooky, and they were both afraid.

That your boyfriend? Pippa whispered, her voice small.

Maybe, Jax replied. If I want him to be.

You get to choose?

Jax shoved her with an elbow.

Don't be an idiot. We always get to choose.

They'd walked quickly, neither of them wanting to be on that dark lane any longer than they had to be, but still it seemed to take ages until they were on the crushed gravel of their driveway. A bathroom light was on upstairs, and the stove light in the kitchen, and as they got closer Jax saw that someone had left the light on in the butler's pantry.

Do we have to climb? her sister whispered then, thinking that the kitchen door would be locked and not sure she could make a climb that high—and not sure what happened when you got to the top. How do you get inside from the roof?

Basement, Jax said confidently. Not that anything's ever locked, but just in case Mum's up.

So Jax had done this before. Pippa dropped her sister's hand, the house starting to loom over them, and Jax sensed what was happening.

If you tell on me, she said sharply, I'll tell on you.

They'll say it's your fault. You're older. You're responsible.

Maybe. But they'll put bars on every window and you'll never get out ever again. Not even when you're George's age.

Pippa thought about that. Their house as a block of prison cells wasn't so hard to believe; their parents' favoured punishment was grounding them.

Fine, she said. But I don't think you should do it again.

Was pretty fun, though, wasn't it? Jax shoved her little sister playfully. Luce looked like he had a good time.

Pippa kicked her shin, and Jax gasped, and at the same moment they saw him—their father—sitting at a table on the patio.

Shit, Jax breathed.

There was no chance of escape because he was standing now and coming out onto the driveway to intercept them, his footsteps crisp on the gravel.

He's been waiting for us, Pippa said.

The whole night was evaporating before this singular moment—caught red-handed sneaking back in.

Where have you been?

He sounded worn out, not angry.

Neither girl answered: Jax too dumbfounded by her father's presence after all those other nights of sneaking out and never being caught, and Pippa too scared.

Go to bed, he said then. Our secret.

They scuttled past him and into the house, not questioning their luck, just wanting to get away before he changed his mind.

That's how he shows his love for us, each sister was thinking as she crept upstairs. By leaving us alone.

In their childhood memories, their father was not a monster. He was, he would tell them, the essential gearing mechanism that underpinned the entire enterprise of their world, and they'd grown up believing that, as children do, each of them trusting in the basic goodness of this man whose love had branded them. And each sister wore her mark in secrecy, for in the accepted narrative of the family their father was an emotional simpleton—incapable of grasping complexity.

Dad, they'd scoff to each other, rolling their eyes. His behaviour a toddler's, his tantrums over the top. And they'd shift to their mother like a tensed phalanx, shields up against the volley of abuse he hurled at them from the pinnacle fortress of his superiority. And they, down there at its base, indulgently just waiting him out. Knowing it would pass and that he was more than that—that these eruptions might be volcanic in their intensity but they blew only ash. Nothing so bad it would entomb them. And their mother—bless her—never buckled. Certainly there were times, when they were teenagers, that the bond between their parents had seemed near to breaking, but the girls' schools were full of broken homes—divorce was typical—and as far as the sisters knew arguments and tinges of violence were the normal patterns of a marriage. And in those teenage years, each girl had her own traumas and mini tragedies. Their parents were just part of the background. Reliably there, and reliably volatile.

The truth, of course, was somewhat different. That night, they'd surprised him too—and when put against what *he* was outside for, their infraction didn't merit punishment. Didn't even warrant consideration. Because upstairs, where he'd left her, his wife—for the first time in many years—was silent. He had made her so, the fact of it laced across his knuckles and the flats of his hands and even his elbows. He didn't know why his elbows were bruised, one of them scraped and bleeding, and even sitting alone under that dark sky, he couldn't work it out.

Jax stretched out on one of the chaise longues in the sun to dry off. The approaching meet up with that old boyfriend had been unplanned—just a coincidence that he should email her out of the blue concerning the very same weekend she'd be back in town. He lived in another country now too, and was back just for a week. How could there be anything illicit about that? And sure as shit, she'd thought, I'll need a break from all this. *This* being the house, the family and whatever histrionics her little sister was going to unleash.

She flexed her toes and crossed both arms over her chest, stretching them, her muscles sore from paddling the day before. Because her last-minute trip to Canada was not a reason, her husband had announced, for all of them to suffer. He'd insisted they stick with their plan for a family paddle in the Gulf of Mexico before dropping her at the airport to make her flight. She couldn't say no, because he'd dangled her sudden trip home as a sort of bargaining chip. *If you get that, then I get this.*

They were a perfect family. Good looking and symmetrical— their children like golden twins, a boy and a girl, exactly two years apart to the day. They were all-American: healthy, home-packed lunches, PTA membership, field trips for enrichment, team sports and a musical instrument. They were the family everyone looked to; the benchmark for how to make it work. Never mind that sometimes the dishes went unwashed until there was nothing left to put a sandwich on. That the same happened with the laundry, with the tables and the couches, with the bedroom floors. That they would find themselves, sometimes, waking to a house so filled with detritus that they would have to spend weeks sorting through it, closing their doors to visitors lest anyone find them out. And all of it Jax's fault because, as well as her job (which was barely even that—a few hours downtown in the library's public relations office), she volunteered in community theatre writing plays that, if they were staged, sent the house and everything in it to hell. Her husband, the source of their steady income—a high school biology teacher—treated it as an experiment. Stood back, observed, and did nothing to help. The conclusion was always the same, the half-life of domestic harmony being constant, and still he did nothing to intervene, as if the natural processes at work were paramount. From the outside, they were the family, and the couple, that you dreamt of being: solid and happy and overflowing with love. From the inside, they often were barely standing.

She'd felt her anger start as the storm rolled in, out at sea. They'd slipped their kayaks under the mangroves to the flooded clearing at the islet's centre because it was calm in there and protected. The sandy bottom was clouded with stingrays like captives in a touch-tank.

What is this place? the kids said. Let's name it!

They named everything. The places their kayaks touched weren't named on maps because they were sandbars that shifted, oyster reefs that grew and fell away, islands that were so barren no one had ever thought they deserved a spot on a map except as a numbered hazard to steer around, and so they named these places for themselves: Drift Dive Point where the current was so strong they could jump in and ride it with the fish, Turtle Island where their son had found the dead sea turtle washed up. Lizard Lagoon, Collision Channel, Crab Cove . . .

Mangrove Millpond? Jax said.

But the children were already shouting out their own names. Stingray Sea. Stingray Shuffle. No. Stingray Council. Let's call it Stingray Council. It's where they meet and decide things like where to hide. Yeah. And how to ambush us, the kids shouted, feet trailing over the side, their hair flaxen coronas, giggling as the rays' pectorals tickled their skin. Afraid of nothing.

Stingray Council, Jax said, bringing her kayak around. Perfect. Daddy, mark it down.

The Gulf had started heaving when they were three miles out. They'd seen the clouds gathering before they launched but had gone out anyway because more often than not summer storms in Florida pass quickly. Not a reason to cancel the day, their last chance to paddle mid-week before school started.

Maybe we should just stay here? Wait it out, she'd said, hooking her hand around a mangrove root to steady her boat.

No, it's fine, her husband replied, reaching for his bag of trail mix, nonchalant, his life jacket undone, his skin bare as if the sun and a sunburn would be fine too.

And a melanoma? she'd wanted to shout. I suppose that would be fine as well.

Her anger was sudden, violent, surprising. But coherent. She wanted to punish him. To ruin his moment, to make him sit up and put his back into it like their little boy had done out there in the waves, to be the man he wasn't, to reward nothing about him until he understood once and for all how it was for her. How easy he had it. How much she'd given him so that he could sit there, unconcerned and confident, the world lying down for him.

With a powerful sweep of her paddle, she'd spun her boat and surged toward the opening and out to sea, leaving him behind.

You'll have to help me, she shouted to her son in the bow seat, grabbing the mangroves to leverage the boat out, the incoming tide trying to keep them in. Hard left, hard left! she yelled as the front of the kayak exited the tunnel. But it was the sea in the end, with a blow, that knocked them toward land. Her husband's boat had come alongside them, closing the gap so there was no water to put her blade into, and she saw him flick his eyes at his biceps as if being strong, being able to propel the boat easily by himself, was the point. As if those muscles, bigger than hers, were something he'd invented rather than something ordained at conception.

It seemed grotesque and repulsive to be this way and she hated him even more for it. With a single stroke her husband's kayak had knifed free of them, straight into the waves, two boat-lengths away already, and they battled on separately, their boats diverging as he arrowed straight for the jutting mainland and the cover of land. Jax had to let the waves and the incoming tide help her press on over the open water, trusting the Gulf to carry her and their son to land.

When she finally reached shore she knew that she'd beaten him. Behind her, just rounding the point and following the shoreline, was her husband's kayak with their daughter huddled up front. She would be cold, no fat on her, lips blue and skin mottled and a foul temper to match, but first this—Jax's obscene glory at having beaten him. For once, having shown him what she could do.

It was when the boats were loaded and they were in the car and ready to leave for the airport, the kids changed and dry and in the back seat reading their books, that her husband started things up again.

I should probably get changed too, he'd said. As if he'd just thought of it, with his hand at the ignition. Do I have anything dry to change into? he asked her. Innocent. Of everything.

Jax imagined taking the driftwood at her feet and pushing it into his face. It was sharp enough, and she had the rage to drive it home. She imagined a foot at his throat. She imagined his hands pinned to the steering wheel. She imagined her children continuing to read.

10

Georgina looked down at her sister lying in the sunshine and thought how lucky she was, that she still looked as fit as when they were teenagers. Even given all the booze and drugs she'd taken, and the two babies—both of whom she'd breastfed for *years*. Jax: always so fucking perfect, and always sure to let you know. Georgina lowered the blind because there'd be more than enough of that in the coming days. More Jax, and how she was better than all of them. She turned back to look at Pippa, still crashed out on the bed, and noted the backpack dropped on the floor and so empty it was pushed halfway under the bed without even scraping the box spring. Evidently she wasn't here to stay. What had their mother even meant? Nothing about this seemed planned out at all.

Margaret was in the kitchen, complaining to herself about

how hot it was and making another attempt at a list for the grocery store because Georgina had let her down by not getting everything she needed. Where was the bag of flour? Or the currants? Where were the tins of tuna fish in olive oil or the saltines? Where, in fact, was that eldest daughter?

She put the kettle on. It was the third time she'd set it to boil without using the water for anything. She opened the cupboard where they kept the cereals as if she might, for the first time in her life in that house, pour a bowl of cornflakes to eat. She was like an automaton, her pattern of movements along pre-set vectors, and when Georgina came in it was to find her mother motionless, smoke swirling from her right hand—a brief pause before starting again: list, kettle, cereal, list, kettle . . .

Pippa's sleeping, Georgina told her, getting past her mother to the other side of the room near the back door, leaning up against the bench.

Well, Margaret answered, you saw yourself what she was like.

And Jax is sunbathing, Georgina said, looking over at the windows fronting the pool. Guess there's not enough sun where she lives.

She's always loved that pool. Go and see if she wants tea, Georgie.

Margaret's tone softening at the thought of all her children in the house again.

And take her a towel. That little girl is always forgetting her towel.

They had their tea out on the porch, the three of them, Margaret listening as Jax talked about what she thought was wrong with

Philippa, discussing the toll the pregnancy had taken, reminding them both that her own pregnancies had been so hard that after the second one she'd sworn off them forever. *And Pip's had five*, Jax said. Georgina sat there thinking what bullshit that was, but not saying anything because it would just give her sister the opening to gloat that having a mere *one* baby didn't qualify you to speak about pregnancy.

Being here will help, Georgina offered up instead. Knowing that was what their mother believed—and their mother smiled, seizing on it.

Yes, she said. Time in your own bed always helps, don't you think? It's important for us to keep things as normal as possible.

So I should steal some of George's clothes? Jax grinned. Or Pip's jewellery?

Just being a family.

Georgina swirled what was left of her tea.

Not sure how Dad's tour fits in with that.

Is that why he asked me to help him in the garden today? Is there a tour group coming?

Tomorrow, Margaret said. Apparently. She flicked her ash over the porch railing. I've told him to cancel it.

The two sisters said nothing, because this was the natural ebb and flow of that household. They knew that once the rancour reached the point it could no longer be contained by a veneer of civility, it would explode and take their parents on that familiar track of violence to acceptance that their marriage was built on—and which they both seemed to need, because the blow-ups always signalled a return to tenderness. A honeymoon that might last for a year.

—

David put Jax to work, as he'd said he would, pulling weeds in the topiary garden. It was adjacent to the terrace where the refreshments would be served and so it was imperative it look perfect, nothing out of place. When the people stood with their cold drinks and canapés, trying to imagine all of this belonging to them, David wanted them to realize they'd never have a chance because absolute beauty such as this was earned, not bestowed—and there was no one who worked harder at that than he.

She'll come around, he'd said when Jax mentioned his wife being unhappy about the tour. She always does. That's her singular talent, isn't it?

He'd smiled, looking at this daughter who was the closest he had to a son, her forthright confidence what he associated with boys. In truth, he loved all his girls—but this one perhaps more.

Do you remember, Jax asked him then as he stooped to pull a weed to show her what she should remove. That time you caught us sneaking back in? Me and Pip? We'd been out all night, she said. She could tell he didn't know what she was talking about, was still bristling with all the unfinished jobs he had to do, his mind focused on the present. On the dandelion in his hand, on setting her up to work effectively.

You never got us in trouble, she said, her tone a mix of admiration and astonishment.

Children, he responded, have one fatal flaw. They believe they are the centre of the universe when in fact, if they exist at all, it's somewhere at the outer limits.

Easier just to let us go, eh?

David shrugged. You always were hard to crack. There was most likely something more pressing I was dealing with.

At four in the morning?

David put the weed in his pocket and slapped both hands against his legs. No harm in a bit of fun, he said, as if he might throw her to the ground and wrestle her. As if they were mates, and he understood, and he was envious. Wishing that night had been his.

And Jax grinned, because here was the father she loved. The man she would always defend because he laced his punishments for her transgressions with the sense that he knew full well why she'd done what she'd done—and he didn't really disapprove. He encouraged it.

Before long, Georgina was out there too, summoned from the house where she'd been lying on her bed in the same clothes she'd arrived in the day before. Taking a moment for herself because she already knew how this day was shaping up and that it would continue to gather confusion until it was a Tower of Babel leaning into its own destruction.

Edging, her father said, leading her to the parterre and instructing her to chisel every rounded inch of it until it was scribed perfectly into the soil.

Like an architect's final plan, he said, handing her the edging tool.

Or a yantra, she replied. Knowing the comparison was well outside his Western frame of reference and thrilling, like a child again, at the momentary pause of his incomprehension before he nodded impatiently.

Yes. That's right, a *yantra*. Sweeping one arm at the scope of the work ahead of her before marching off to another part of the garden, out of sight.

And collect the turf, he called back. Toss it over.

Like all the sisters, Georgina was familiar with the various gardening tools and how to use them, having spent many paid and unpaid hours working these grounds. And she knew that the rhythmic plunge-tilt-leverage of edging was less taxing than a lot of other jobs her father could have given her—like the weeding he'd stuck her sister with—and as long as she stayed focused and kept the garden's shape, didn't wobble, here was another chance to rest. To think about things, clear her mind, to just let the hypnotic repetition of the movements at the border of this impossibly beautiful grouping of flowers ease her tension. Because she had something to work out, if only she could let it come to the surface. Some problem of her own, she suspected, even if she couldn't name it. But it was there, like a blister forming.

Georgina toiled until there was enough sod cut for her to stoop and bundle it up, a shedding crumbling dirty armful pressed to her chest, the smell of it strangely appealing because her hunger for something like this, for something tangible, was keen. When was the last time she'd handled anything real? The flowers had been a start, but her mother had ruined that. Here, her father was giving her another chance.

Margaret, standing in one of the living room windows, watched Georgina as she walked around the terrace, past the topiary, and out of sight to the cliff, where Margaret knew she'd throw the sod over the fence. Where they threw everything they didn't need anymore. She turned her attention to the clipped hedges where her other daughter was, her body appearing every so often to stand up and stretch. *That one's approach never as diligent as Georgie's.* And Margaret found herself filled then with such a sudden love for these imperfect girls that when Georgina reappeared and stopped a moment to talk with Jax, Margaret went to the terrace door to call them in so that she could wrap them, like babies, in her arms and smother them. But by the time she'd fiddled with the key and turned it in the lock, they were gone: Jax to the weeds, and Georgina out front with one knee cocked above the foot plate of the edging tool, back at work.

Darling, Margaret called out from the terrace, fluttering her hand at Georgina. Wanting to draw her back. Knowing that Jax, at the sound of her mother's voice, would have sunk even lower to the ground to hide. That Georgina would be more likely to come.

I need help, Margaret explained. Something I can't do by myself, Georgie.

But it was not just a single task she had in mind, it was a whole long inexhaustible made-up list of them to keep Georgina out of the garden until David noticed that she'd abandoned her post and defected back to the house. His wife, resisting him.

Georgina! he'd yell from the doorstep, into the house, pulling her back outside. I need you *out here.*

And so the afternoon went. Even Jax, who was so practised at evasion, was included in her parents' tug-of-war between house and grounds, a string of half-finished jobs she and Georgina kept being brought back to and told to complete. And rather than voice their mounting frustration they turned it on the chores, attacking them with an intensity that took even their parents by surprise. Making them wonder, for an instant, who these women were . . . before immediately relegating them to childhood again. Unruly wayward girls who needed marshalling. And, perhaps even more than that, batons to be passed and sometimes dropped.

Ordering Chinese in for dinner was Jax's idea but no one objected, least of all Georgina. Everything ached, and she was happy to pass the cooking chore to someone else. David, with his usual sigh of persecution, gave his credit card over but refused to cover the tip. To pay for *every*thing. And when a teen arrived with the cartons of food and, when instructed to, brought them through the house and set them sullenly on the kitchen island, and when Georgina gave the boy cash for his efforts and when, without even looking at the amount, he shoved the bills into his back pocket and left without saying *any*thing, David felt entirely justified when he proclaimed:

Owner's son. Being taught a thing or two.

As if this was a lesson to them.

But his family was already filling their plates with food, unwilling to acknowledge whatever the moral was he was trying to illuminate. Even Pippa was there, scooping food onto her plate and following the others out to the porch where they would all sit in the failing light of day's end and, because of the informality of eating on their laps and tucking their feet up on the wicker furniture, not have to talk. Not have to do anything except eat and get more, and eat again. Settle back deep into their weariness to convalesce.

Saturday

11

The next morning they came not as you would think, in a group, but as a trickle. No fanfare preceded their taking of the grounds, and at first Georgina thought those flashes of colour were birds or fantastic butterflies until she saw one, intact, in the clearing near the obelisk fountain. A man, wearing Bermuda shorts and a brightly patterned shirt, dipping his hand into the water and rubbing it across the base of his neck. She watched him bend right down, like an ibis. Like those toys they'd had as kids, perched on the edge of their drinking glasses, counterweighted geegaws with a top hat. Was he *drinking* it? Surely he realized the water was recirculated, not potable. That it was just another pretty feature of the garden. That there wasn't a natural water source for miles.

David had seen them too, through the window. Looking up from his accounts to rest his eyes on all his staggering achievements outside, he had seen, instead, the affront of their presence there—he looked at his watch—two *hours* ahead of schedule. He wasn't even dressed. He was still drinking his second cup of tea and his wife was still in bed—none of the refreshments were ready—and he'd planned on doing a final check of all the paths to make sure there weren't still piles of weeds or trimmings to clear away. Tearing out of the living room, he wrenched the front door, not even pausing to close it, just letting it hang open like an invitation to come in. His footsteps were quick as a horse in harness and became a canter when he began to see even more people drifting between flower beds, their heads intermittently visible above rose bushes, on the far side of the tennis court between the clematis, or standing up after having crouched to examine something in the herbaceous border . . . they were everywhere and nowhere, like hummingbirds. A swarm. An infestation.

Excuse me, David called out imperiously to a figure crossing the driveway thirty feet ahead, because this would never do. These people must be reined in and organized so he could give the talk he'd prepared and take them through the garden himself. It was vital they followed a certain order when viewing the grounds or they'd miss the whole ruddy point of them. Miss the sheer brilliance of what he'd scraped from the earth with his own bare hands and fashioned into the all-important fretwork that elevated him from simple county seat to principality. This wasn't just a *garden*, he thought, spitting and indignant. He must make them understand that it was a meticulously crafted symphony like none they'd ever experienced.

But the woman didn't even falter. She just walked into the cover of the rhododendrons as if David wasn't there, and so stealthily that when he got to the place where she'd disappeared there was no sign of her. Not even a leaf quivering. He looked around wildly but he could see nothing that resembled authority. No bus idling on the lane, its driver paid to wait, or man at the gate counting heads . . . no one at all to unleash his anger on. It was as though the people were materializing out of the soil because as he stood, and spun, unsure how to proceed, David spied increasing numbers of them but none of them close enough to take hold of and shake.

Margaret, he thought bitterly. She's changed the start time and not told me.

And then he saw, ducking into the lilac copse and within shouting distance, a couple who'd clearly seen him too because he recognized their movements from his own children: subterfuge and deceit. They were running away from him.

Oi!

He strode after them, but when he got there, the only figure beneath the arching lilacs was the life-sized statue of Aphrodite he'd placed there years ago like a private viewing booth. And she, of course, would never speak to him. Couldn't tell him what was happening, or where they'd gone or what they'd been conspiring about with their heads tipped together as they scurried out of sight. He peered out into the sunlit spaces and wondered, for an instant, if he'd imagined the couple . . . but then he saw a black rectangle moving across the lawn, followed by the white triangle of a woman's skirt. They were heading for the terrace.

Party crashers. Philistines. Uncultured barbarians, just here for the food.

You there!

He followed the mulched path out of the copse and charged directly across the lawn to the shaded terrace, which was, he couldn't help noticing, resplendent with the hydrangeas he'd planted in front of it. *Hydrangea aspera* subsp. *sargentiana*—each purple bloom a triumph. They'd been a special order he'd coaxed to maturity, thirty-one of them planted like an elongated bolster of richness and texture to soften the terrace's low wall where it met the grass. Over the years he'd probably replaced every plant at least once until he'd chanced on individual ones that were hardy enough to withstand the brutal winters in that exposed location, but it had been worth it because there, in front of him, were the results. His perseverance, he believed, had blended with the root stock to make them invincible in their splendour. And even in his current predicament, he couldn't help feeling a flush of pride.

David's slippers and the hem of his dressing gown were becoming saturated with dew and he had a moment where he felt ridiculous, out there on the lawn in his pyjamas, but his anger quickly stifled that and instead he thought if he could just catch *one* of them he could get to the bottom of what was happening. He still had time to make it right. But when he gained the terrace and found it empty, David knew he'd been wrong about that couple. Their evasive manoeuvres smacked of strategy.

This is an attack, he thought. *Not an impulsive jaunt. And they've caught us by surprise.*

As he stood on the terrace, at the top of its wide granite steps, something else caught his attention. His wife, waving frantically from one of their bedroom windows on the second floor. David dropped his eyes, intent on ignoring her, even when she rapped on the glass so hard he thought she'd break it and her sharp little fist would come through to try for him. Whatever it was it could wait because he blamed her for all of this, and he'd be buggered if he'd give her the satisfaction of seeing his distress.

Georgina stepped out of the house just then, opening her mouth to speak.

Not now, David snapped at her, flapping a hand, hurrying down the other set of steps that led through the yew hedge and into the formal white garden. Thinking that surely the man's black shirt would be obvious here, even if the woman blended with the garden's theme. But this garden was empty too, only the Lutyens bench at one end and the twelve-foot-high hedges pruned into battlements surrounding the partitioned flower beds. Each of the four sides had openings tunnelled into the yews, and David hesitated, unsure which way he should go, listening for some kind of clue, but this garden was so secluded and well muffled that all he could hear was his own laboured breathing.

Dad, Georgina called out from the terrace, putting her head through the hedge.

And then the rapping again, on an upstairs window.

What is it?

He spat the words out, flame and sparks.

There's a phone call for you.

Can't you take a message?

He turned to look at this eldest daughter who didn't have the sense to realize what a critical moment this was, and then up at his wife who was hovering at their bathroom window now—thinking that the apple doesn't fall far from the fucking tree.

It's the tour leader, Georgina said flatly. On the phone. In the kitchen.

Well why didn't you say so, David huffed, as he hurried onto the terrace and past his daughter and through the entire length of the house as if it were only a long corridor littered with obstacles. His slippers leaving wet grassy smudges on the oak floors.

He picked up the receiver. Yes, he said. Dr. Blackford here.

By the time Georgina arrived back in the kitchen the conversation was over and her father was standing there next to the laundry chute door, next to the wall-mounted phone, next to the drawers with the cutlery and the everyday napkins trying, just trying, to take it in.

The bus has broken down, he said. So he has sent the group on ahead, by foot, while he waits for another to be brought in.

How long will that take?

Hours, David said. It will take—hours.

He looked out the nearest window, to the pool with its effusive plantings, and saw a neon orange baseball cap moving just above the greenery. He shuddered. A baseball cap.

Hours, he repeated quietly to himself. And they will trample everything. This was the *second* garden on their schedule, he said, but because the bus broke down within walking distance of it they . . .

This was not how it was supposed to go. Not at all what he'd planned.

Darling, Margaret said silkily from the kitchen doorway where she'd been standing, waiting for the perfect moment to drop the nasty little cherry bomb she'd been readying. There is a very young couple back in the topiary, undressing one another. Clear as day. I did try to tell you, she said.

—

Margaret knew exactly what she was doing. Her husband's mood, ever since word of Pippa coming home, had been intensifying, and she was well aware of what it would take to bring it back down. Knew that when there was too much happening all at the same time, it challenged David's belief that he was in control. Typically, Margaret would bear the brunt of his mania in order to keep the household together. She'd lie down and take the blows he needed to land to feel powerful again, but with Pippa—. Now she wouldn't be as available for that. All her focus needed to be on Pippa, and she couldn't afford to be sidelined by one of his bouts of insecurity.

It was a half-formed thought, an instinct more than anything, but she knew her husband's fondness for pretty girls, and if she could just set him on a course for the one who'd presented herself so unexpectedly—a golden opportunity—he might just direct his fury there and spare the rest of them. Leave them to get on with the matter at hand, which wasn't his crack-up of a tour but the very real crisis of Pippa in jeopardy.

12

Actual figures—people, animals, fantastical beasts—escaped him. The best David could do was shapes, and so the topiary garden he'd created was a geometric confection in all the shades of green, from the lime of boxwood to the malachite of arborvitae. And because of that the two people at the centre of it, partially shielded by the extravagantly tapering spiral of an Alberta spruce, were immediately obvious even from the second-floor window where David had gone, at his wife's urging, to see for himself. Their skin gleamed like Pentelic marble and they were as lusty and swollen as the plantings were chiselled. Their movements—jerky and quick—gave away what they were doing and so David, taking in this new outrage, turned for the stairs and returned to the terrace. Once outside he slowed, but he needn't have, because the couple was too engaged to notice anything beyond each other's bodies. He watched, mesmerized, trying to work out the details of how they were fitted together. Focusing, finally, on the orbs of the girl's breasts, which—bent over as she was—seemed much too big and too round to go with those narrow shoulders and the winsome face turned up and slightly to one side, as if she were trying to see who was behind her. And then David realized the man was pulling her, his hand grasping her hair. Rough. He recognized that desire to dominate.

He must have lurched or cried out, because they saw him then and dropped out of sight and all that was left was the garden and that same perfect scene he'd looked at a million times but which was now, suddenly, not nearly enough. David descended onto the pathway and waded in among the topiary, looking for them, unable to stop himself, the garden's horde of marauders forgotten for the moment as he fixated on this arousing improbability of a young couple having sex in his garden. And as he approached he could hear whispering and the scrape of gravel as they pulled their clothes back on, bickering, and he imagined them blaming each other for stopping before they'd finished. For being too loud or too vigorous, for attracting attention, the man's voice elevated and angry now and the girl silenced by it. By the time David got to the spruce, the only sign of the couple was the disturbed ground and a strapless bra which, in their panic, had been left behind. Too complicated, David guessed, fingering its flimsy red prettiness. Or too torn. He scanned the grounds, above and between the stacked cubes and evergreen sentry cones and balled holly, and couldn't help thinking about those breasts that were unencumbered now and crawling away from him. And how deliciously close he'd been to having them.

He quickened his step, choosing one path after another, but the couple had vanished like fauna out there somewhere on his land. He remembered the white triangle and black square but all he could see were the flashy colours of others wandering the garden, getting in the way. Nothing but impediments now—a sea of red herrings to slow him down. He returned to the slight rise near the terrace and stood there, searching in every direction for the girl who'd escaped him, knowing she should be easy to see in this crowd because she was a butterfly to all those beetles. She was a swan to their geese, and he wanted her.

No one knew this garden better than he did. He would flush her out.

David headed for the thickets and groves where he knew the man would be finishing what he'd started in the topiary—because David had the same urgency. The same absolute need to conquer what was weakest. Would have been doing exactly that if it had been him and he'd had the opportunity. And as he walked faster and faster he resolved, when he found them, to push the man aside and take the girl for himself. Take, by virtue of this being his land, what was rightfully his.

But they were everywhere, the tourists. A skulk of them in the lilacs with Aphrodite, sitting on the bench and staring vacantly. Another group meandering through the cedar boundary hedge he'd planted in a double row for privacy. A few glanced at him suspiciously, this man in his silk dressing gown and slippers, but it wasn't until he entered the tennis court to cross to the apple trees that someone grabbed his arm.

You live here? the woman said, scrutinizing his pyjamas.

When he tried to slip away, she clamped her other hand onto him as if he were a life preserver in heavy seas.

We need things, she said.

He looked at her then. The white visor, the frosted hair, the heavy gold Gucci chain peeking out from her neck folds—not a woman to be trifled with. He knew, at one glance, that this woman could package him up and deliver him to hell without breaking a sweat.

I know, he said, letting his arm go limp. We all need things.

She moved closer. So close he could see the creases in her makeup and feel the padded points of her chest, too spongy to be natural, against his upper arm through the silk and the Egyptian cotton of his pyjamas.

We want value for our money. Not—she let one hand go and grabbed a spent bloom off the fence—*this*. What the *fuck* is this.

The word so vulgar and unexpected it startled him. David tried projecting what she wanted him to be—Christ Pantocrator, Zeus Xenios—but it came across as disdain and made her grip on his arm even tighter. He knew there'd be marks, and that he didn't deserve this and that now was not the time because he had other quarry to subdue. And so he became, in that instant, an embodiment of conciliation and charm—the doddering lord of the manor, emasculated and ready to help, offering to give a personal tour of all the triumphs she'd so obviously ("and tragically") missed . . . until she released him, just enough, that he could twist and be free.

He darted across the court, knowing she wouldn't follow, because she was a mannequin. A sheep in wolf's clothing, a ruse sent to keep him from his prey. But he wouldn't be deterred. Nose to the ground, he disappeared into the shrubbery to pick up the scent, criss-crossing every flower bed, mown path and clump of trees and even entering the coach house and going upstairs to the low sloping room to look for them among the rat droppings. But the garden—if it still had them—wasn't giving them up.

David stood in the middle of the drive, looking back at the house, immobile with hurt that his wife had done this to him. Had compromised the tour and then pretended to hand him something he couldn't have. Teasing and destroying him in one fell blow. After all the many things he'd given her, she would begrudge him even this. Hadn't he given in to *everything* and asked for *nothing* in return? Unless—the thought struck him—this was a game. One of those elaborate scenarios she liked to build around sex, murmuring the details when he was pounding her in their bedroom late at night. Could she have arranged this? A tryst? A lark? And the hurt, then, was replaced with gratitude at the possibility of that which, in his desperation, became more and more real. Attainable. Believable.

Their mother was in such a state when Jax came downstairs and entered the kitchen, still half-asleep, that she didn't even say hello.

Butter, was what Margaret said. It's the butter I'm out of, and how can I get some now with the garden so overrun? Oh. Darling—

Growing butter now, huh? Jax said cheekily, looking over at Georgina and rolling her eyes.

I wouldn't go out there, Margaret said, noting Jax's bathing suit. They're everywhere.

And before Jax could reply, there was a knock on the door. And before Margaret could tell her not to, Jax had opened it.

The answer to what her mother was talking about was standing there: a late-middle-aged woman in a print sundress with sagging spaghetti straps, demanding a glass of iced water, stepping inside without being asked, glaring at Margaret, Jax and Georgina as if the heat was all their fault (how *dare* you), leaning against the counter, waiting to be handed a glass. Tapping—*tapping*—her foot.

They said there would be refreshments, the woman said. We were counting on that.

Jax looked helplessly at her mother, but Margaret was busy rooting through the refrigerator, her head and shoulders behind its open door and both arms inside pushing food around on the shelves, looking for butter.

Water? Georgina said. Yes, of course. It is hot out there, isn't it?

But the woman wasn't interested in small talk; she only wanted, after a moment to catch her breath, to unload all her grievances about how utterly mismanaged this day had been *already* and still three more gardens to go, assuming they could scare up a functioning bus to take them all . . . And as she gulped the cold water Georgina handed her, the comments became more expansive and she talked about the need for *two* buses because they'd been so overcrowded on that first one, and how she was sure it had broken down because of the sheer human weight it had been made to carry. Some of them, she said, were such *heifers* they took up two whole seats apiece.

She stared hard at each of them, making sure they'd heard, as if there was somehow something wrong with them that their garden, their property, should attract such grotesquery. And as if *she* was somehow separate from that.

Margaret and her two daughters felt passingly stunned by this woman's barrage and they each stood there, dumb, thinking what came most naturally to them. Jax: what a delicious comedy. Georgina: what an unnecessary burden, on top of everything else. And Margaret: what a shambles from the start, and here was the proof.

And furthermore, the woman continued, holding her glass out to Georgina for more water, they refused to refund my husband's ticket even though I told them he wasn't—

But Georgina had snapped into action and with a single deft movement she ushered the woman out onto the porch and down to the drive and across the gravel to where the mown path started in, keeping up a steady patter of words in her effort to get this woman away from the house and back out where she must stay until the bus came to take her, and the rest of them, away. This, at least, was something that Georgina could control.

Near the weeping pussy willow they encountered two men bent right down to the ground, fiddling with the shrub's base, and the woman realized an instant before Georgina that they were taking a cutting. She drew her breath in, incensed, and thrust her head forward like a chicken getting ready to peck at this outrageous liberty. Georgina, seizing the opportunity, backed away, because the woman had something new to fixate on now— either upbraiding or joining them in this bad behaviour. And anyway, Georgina thought, looking around, *one hundred cuttings couldn't decimate this.*

But as she passed by the Yulan magnolia and moved through the circular herb garden with its brick walkways and around the tall stone obelisk, she began to wonder if the tour numbers were increasing because there were people everywhere. Ghosting through the property, lost in their own perceptions of it, some drifting en masse and others staring hard at a single bloom like herons waiting for a tremor of movement before striking. And many of them, she began to notice, were carrying bouquets of flowers they'd snapped off as if this tour had left them in the wilderness and they were free to pick what they liked. Pick, discard and pick again—because even the clearings, she saw, were strewn with dying blooms in every shade and colour. They were stripping things.

Her father would be livid when he saw this. And where was he? Wasn't he meant to be leading them? This tour had no shape, and these people didn't fit neatly in any one category. They weren't a civic or special interest group—their behaviour was too erratic. They looked at the plants and they swatted them; they collected and discarded them; some were dressed for the midway and others for the mall. And most of them didn't even look old enough to want to spend a morning doing this. It was a retirees' game, these garden tours, but these people—she passed two near the asters—could have been plucked from the sidelines of a soccer match. Middle-aged men and women who seemed as bewildered to be there as Georgina was to encounter them.

And then she saw her father, back in the topiary, stalking the trimmed hedges. She could tell, by the rigid set of his shoulders, that he was furious and looking for a perpetrator, and Georgina knew she should help him because nobody else was going to, but instead she returned to the house. She could say she was there for Philippa. And wasn't that the truth? She knew, from long experience, that her father's trajectory was gaining speed and she didn't want to be around when he ignited.

—

Margaret was still talking about the cake. Still rattling off the ingredients and saying she needed eggs and butter.

And your father—she levelled her eyes at Jax—is no help at all.

Tell me about it, Jax replied with exaggerated surrender, putting a mug of coffee into the microwave to reheat. My husband, she said, is useless too.

But Margaret wasn't listening. She was distracted by the thought of David out there in the garden with that couple having sex, which she knew was where it was heading when she'd seen the man rip the girl's top from her back. Nothing about sex was new to Margaret, but she was second-guessing having practically led her husband to it, because it could all swing back so horribly down on top of her.

I can go, Jax said, stirring sugar into her coffee, leaning against the counter and watching her mother to gauge the morning's temperament. To the store, she smiled innocently. She was thinking of the boy and their plans and that she might buy a new colour for her hair, or some lip gloss, or eyeliner—or any one of the many other frivolous purchases she used to add on to her mother's credit card when sent to the grocery store as a teen.

What was that? Margaret murmured, because she was having trouble following any line of thought except the one involving her husband.

Uggh!

Margaret cried out as if she'd been hit, because behind Jax an enormous man stepped through from the family room.

Toilet, he said, like a caveman. Like someone for whom language was irrelevant.

Even Jax was startled. A sonic boom, right in her ear.

What—?

He was all the way in now, and moving toward the sink.

Can we help you? Jax said, recovering. Her mother had fallen back against the stove.

Toilet, he repeated, his tone so low it scraped the ground and delivered itself up jammed with earth and rocks.

How did you get in? Margaret whispered.

He motioned behind him to deep inside the house, and Jax noticed the vinyl bag hanging from his arm like a purse. On anyone else it would have been a shoulder tote.

Yes, Jax said with a false brightness, painfully aware she was standing there in nothing but a two-piece bathing suit. Straight through and on your right.

And then they watched him leave, blocking out the sun for a moment, back the way he'd come. To the powder room he'd never fit into and then, presumably, out the front door that was beside it—beneath the oak lintel and over the ancient bluestone threshold that seemed just the right tread for a giant.

They looked at each other then, and Jax laughed.

Is it a *circus* tour? she snorted, snapping the back of her bikini bottom against her legs.

I told him to cancel it, her mother said, looking fearful. Told him it would put us all at risk. He should have listened. I knew he should have listened.

13

There were four of them in the swimming pool now. They'd laid their hats and cameras on a table in the shade, and their walking shoes and socks were lined up beside the shallow end's steps, and they were floating fully clothed—Pippa could see them—on their backs, like giant autumn leaves.

Who are they? Are they alive?

She watched them collect on the far side where the garden was closest to the pool's edge and tip themselves upright, in a row, elbows on the concrete pool deck, their faces inches from the flowers which, she could tell, even from her room upstairs, were trembling with bees.

She leaned her forehead against the glass. Did she know them? They weren't her sisters. Nor her mother, who didn't even know how to swim . . . And as Pippa tried to work it out, two more flung themselves in, diving and twisting like porpoises. She watched as the four at the edge turned, in unison, and began pulling themselves hand over hand around the edge and back to the steps and out, like flotsam being pushed by this rogue tide that had risen from god knows where with a pull stronger than the sum of them.

They were lovers, these new ones. Pippa saw it immediately. And naked. She spread both hands out on the glass and her despair was sudden and physical. When was the last time she'd done anything like that? She watched them curl around each other and sink to the bottom, not even needing the air to breathe, existing just for that moment. Staying under longer than seemed possible.

Pippa turned away before they exploded through the surface, and so she missed the terror on one and the laughter on the other. She'd seen only the joy and abandon, and not the way the man had held his girl down to the point of drowning.

David decided that he needed a moment to take stock of things. He needed to get dressed, *and* he needed to take stock of things. Try to ascertain what exactly was going on with this tour turned romp and how he could make it serve him; that couple still out there, he knew, and captive for now with no transportation out.

He slipped along the back side of the woodland garden, along the fence line, crouching under limbs and stepping around shrubs and saplings, pressing wildflowers beneath his feet with each step and feeling, all in all, unfairly treated. That he should be reduced to this—to creeping through his own grounds and making a break for his own house—seemed fundamentally wrong. Everything was off-kilter and unreal. Was he hallucinating? Was this some sort of excessively vivid waking dream? He thought that if he could only get inside and up to his bedroom and out of these pyjamas and into his clothes, then he would feel normal again. Back on top, in charge, not like this—because these were the movements of a scavenger, not a predator. He was slick with sweat, his pyjamas bunching up between his legs and along his thighs as he walked. He felt his chest with both hands and that was damp too, even through his dressing gown—which would be ruined now, stained and puckering. Every weed he hadn't pulled seemed to have thrown itself at him, and he could feel their bristling stickers all along his leg hairs.

It will be cool inside, he told himself. Impatient and eager, now that the house was in sight.

He broke from the perennials for the terrace (still no refreshments, he saw, irritated that he was still the only one working) and then, as quickly as he could, across to the door that led into the living room. *Almost inside.* He turned the knob and pushed but the door didn't open. The blasted frame had swollen in the summer heat. Not until he put his hip and leg against it and tried again, with brute force, did it pop open, and he could step inside and push it shut behind himself. And it was then, after locking the door, that he heard the murmur of unfamiliar voices in the living room.

What the—

It was a family group seated comfortably on the furniture— father, mother, teenage son—so comfortable, so at ease, that David stood and stared at them as if it were he who'd blundered into *their* house. The son was hunched over five different remote control wands, which he'd picked up from various places about the room or possibly the house, and he was pushing buttons and trying to make the stereo turn on. Busily emptying out batteries, switching them around, trying to make them work. David watched as the boy placed a battery between his teeth and bit into it before putting the dented cylinder back into a remote to try again. He'd already rifled through David's CD collection, even shifting the stereo and its custom-made cabinet away from the wall to check all the wires in the back, muttering that the rich old fuck who owned it, and had nothing but pretentious operas and violins on disc, probably hadn't wired the thing properly at the get-go, because what could the owner of all this old shit know about electronics. And not even, he'd sneered, cutting-edge tech. Just top-of-the-line, run-of-the-mill bullshit.

Your house? the man asked David affably, taking in the pyjamas and slippers. Listen, buddy, I was looking over your accounts and you're paying way too much for everything. I'm an accountant, he said—as if his credentials nullified the transgression.

You know, there's a nursery, his wife interjected. Out past the highway. It sells plants marked down to half their price. Some sort of rehab program, I think, for retarded adults.

Developmentally delayed, the son corrected her. Smirking.

And you can claim certain improvements on your taxes every year, the man continued. That tennis court, pool and little garagey house out there—buddy, you could call it a country club. That sets you up for all kinds of savings right there. And that's not even the half of it.

The man was in front of the fireplace now, an elbow resting on the mantel right next to the delicate clock whose timepiece was nested in whip-thin sprays of porcelain flowers. So baroque it was over the top. So fragile, a sudden movement would obliterate it. His blocky arm, squeezed out through the sleeve of his faded pink golf shirt, was moving like a windshield wiper as he used gestures to underline his message that David had been shovelling all his money onto a gigantic bonfire of unnecessary spending. And wasn't it lucky for him that they'd come along when they had? That's called added value for your money right there, he chuckled. Because sure—he sucked air through his teeth, indicating the room they were in—you've got a cushion, but that doesn't mean you need to eat your capital. What are your taxes like? Bet they're high, even with the exemption. Fucking taxman, eh? See now, he said, flexing his back against the fireplace. That's where you'll be able to claw your money back. Taxes. Do you have anyone doing your books? he asked, not missing a beat, because he'd had his start in timeshare sales and he'd been good at it, even if what he'd been selling were ski chalets on a modest hill eighty miles south of the snowbelt. "An all-season vacation home" was how he'd pitched them, which was also the defence he gave when his clients came back in January to nix the deal because the slopes were still green.

Blackford, isn't it? I'll call you David. Listen, David, it's your solvency I'm worried about. Anyone with Accounting 101 can see that your liquidity's all right but you need to be looking long-term. I mean—he snorted—we're not getting any younger. Am I right?

Speak for yourself, dear, his wife said. He's in excellent shape. Aren't you, David? I'll bet you can still run a six-minute mile—Oh, Christ, the son muttered—without even breaking a sweat, she continued.

She had twisted herself up against the couch's arm so that her ample chest was pushed out and her narrow hips cocked to one side, but David wasn't looking at her or the husband or the son. He was staring at the table and at his files, which had been shuffled and opened and spread out like a deck of cards.

I hope you don't mind, the man said, tracking David's gaze. I'm just trying to help, you know. Nice place like this—would be a shame to lose it because you weren't adequately prepared.

And then he reached into the breast pocket of his shirt and pulled out a business card from the small stack he'd put there that morning—*you never know*—and it was that single small fluid movement which finally broke David open.

He didn't know what to address first, there were so many violations unravelling in front of him. He went to the table and methodically closed every single file folder and then he turned, squaring himself to the room, and blasted them with a volley of such foul language that only the teenage boy could actually appreciate the full arsenal.

The tour, David decreed loudly and in all directions, is over.

The tourists left just as they'd come. Silently. Vacuumed up by the shiny red bus that had backed down the entire length of the lane, clipping overhanging branches and dropping into potholes as if its tires had suddenly deflated, until it wedged itself between the gateposts. No one came to the house to ask for the garden's owner, to extend a thank you or an apology or any other ritual of polite society. Rather, it was as if everyone involved wanted to sneak away, as if the whole thing had never happened—an embarrassment on both sides.

Except that it *had* happened, and the proof was everywhere. In the rutted ground, and the broken flower stems and blooms dropped willy-nilly across the landscape like offerings. Someone had made a chain of shasta daisies and tossed it high up over the obelisk, where it had caught jauntily, partway down on the granite, interrupting the water that usually sheeted the obelisk's sides so that now it ran in pretty rivulets, arrhythmic and unpredictable. The pool was spotted with debris—leaves and twigs, a handful of grass clippings flung like confetti—and throughout the entire garden hung the feeling of a gathering just departed. The movement of bodies still present in the air, in the way the plants were slowly straightening themselves to the sun and the grass blades were springing back up, and in the absence of birds and tiny whirring things as the animals waited, just a few moments more, to make sure that the coast was clear.

Inside, the family was hiding too. The tour had been an unprecedented disaster and every one of them knew that there was bound to be a reckoning. And David, already beginning to refortify, knew that something was owed to him.

14

They'd both known it would come. The violence was a periodic necessity of their life together, like a climate oscillation—a prolonged freeze hit by a sudden thaw. And that it came at night, and on the heels of the tour, was no surprise either, because that was how it always was between David and his wife. Neither of them would ever attach the word "rape" to it, because they were married after all and she let him do it. The triggers were predictable and Margaret never shied from them. This time she'd even precipitated it, which fit neatly with David's conviction that she enjoyed it too. Was eager to submit and take the thrashing he delivered. They had, he believed, an understanding that worked for each of them.

The garden tour, he'd thought as he'd pushed himself off her back that night, was a triumph after all. The young girl would have been better, there was no denying it, but he could still imagine her whimperings in the submissive cries of his wife. And that, after all, was better than nothing. It would see him through for a while. Margaret had sworn that the girl wasn't her doing—*Just a coincidence*—but that had only aroused him further. The randomness; the dumb luck. The electrifying tease of live pornography in his very own territory.

David stretched out on his back and took the bed, secure in the knowledge that this was a reset. Whatever debts had accrued were now settled, and the unencumbered life could begin anew.

Margaret, as she always did when it was over, had gone downstairs to wander between rooms until she found herself in the library. She sat at the desk, gingerly, a sheet of sticky dots in front of her. Outside, the storm that had arrived after dark was ferocious. The library windows were rattling, her reflection in them distorted by rain, and the table lamp she switched on wasn't bright enough and Margaret could feel her eyes straining as she debated with herself whether or not to use a colour code. There were blue, orange, yellow, white and red sticker dots, and so she could assign a colour to each child: red dots could be Georgina, blue ones Jax and etcetera.

But what if they forgot or she forgot to tell them? No. Safer, she decided, just to label them with letters.

She sat at the library desk and began marking the stickers with Gs, Js, and Ps, having already decided that she would place them on the bottoms of everything and then no one would have to guess. When she and David died, all the girls would have to do was read the sticker to know if the thing was theirs or not.

She considered the lamp. It was porcelain, Chinese, a gold dragon in a field of turquoise, its base dark lacquered wood. They'd bought it years and years ago at a market in Australia, a sort of antique market near the Brisbane docks. She looked down at the dots in front of her. *P* for Pippa. She peeled it off and stuck the white sticker underneath, next to where the cord came out, wincing because her shoulder hurt. Something about this lamp seemed right for Philippa. That girl needed a dragon. She needed turquoise and beauty and pools of light. Margaret took more objects and stickered them, focused: a tray of meerschaums, prints of da Vinci's sketches, alabaster eggs . . . she didn't bother keeping count, tallying things equally for each girl; she just let her feelings guide her, believing she knew what they'd want, what was best for them. She was their mother, after all. If she couldn't do that then what *could* she do? What had all of it been for? Didn't she know them better than anyone?

Margaret left the library, pausing because she thought she heard sounds in the kitchen, but decided it was just the house bending to the storm. She went through to the living room, raising vases and figurines and bowls and paintings—anything a sticker would adhere to—knowing she'd have to do something about the textiles. The rugs and cushions and throws, even the furniture would need labels. Maybe those tags you iron on clothes when your kids go off to camp. Surely they still made those? She circled around the table with her husband's papers heaped and sliding across it, thankful that at least it wasn't a train set he was obsessing over like so many other men his age. Or a battlefield. Wasn't that something else retired men did as they aged? Glued regiments and artillery onto tables, creating re-enactments of history's most aggressive moments? Some kind of displaced virility. She laughed, girlish, putting a sticker on the underside of the table—a G for Georgina, the only one with a house this table might fit in. They'd had her wedding lunch at this table. Margaret could still see the pretty cake she'd made, chocolate-coated rose petals dusting the platter she'd set it on, three diminishing layers of orange cake with lemon icing, and almond slivers in a chevron around its edges.

Hadn't they always, all of them, been a family? she thought.

Margaret touched her cheek but she wouldn't admit it was wet, the tears streaming now. Or that the salt stung the split corner of her mouth. Instead, she wiped her hand against her leg and moved on to the sideboard with its cupboards of porcelain and silver. A *P* on the silver candlesticks, a *P* on the Waterford crystal, a *P* on the carved ivory birds of paradise even though Pippa had always yelled about the elephants who'd been butchered to make them. At a certain point, Margaret wanted her to know, you just have to give in. Fight will only take you so far and then there's a settling. You have to accept, and move on.

Upstairs, David lay on his side in the oversized bed he sometimes shared with his wife, curled up like a boy. He always lay like this, drawn in on himself; protective, clenched. Nothing woke him. The sleep of the innocent was how he thought of it: the lamb-like slumber of righteousness. If he had dreams he never remembered them and he was thankful for that because they'd only be a distraction from the real work at hand, which was to get himself through the day and acquit himself admirably. To be an example to all. *Ductus exemplo*. There were enough detours already without importing half-realized narratives. Those, he left to his wife, who was off somewhere now, in the middle of the night, doing precisely that, he was sure of it. Taking what was straightforward and simple and strong, and doing her utmost to weaken it. David sighed. Tired. Already nodding off. Already rewriting the slight wobble of the garden tour in lines of hexameter.

But tonight—the storm? Pippa being there? that last piece of cake before bed? something about the accounts?—tonight he was restless. His was a twilight sleep, just barely under, as if he sensed the movement in the house and was fighting—against all previous experience and resolutions—to . . . what? Stop it before it gathered strength? Direct its course? Join this current that ran so deep it coursed through the timber floors and up the walls and shook the mattress . . . ? No, he was struggling to ignore it, not rise up and greet it. Not enter whatever king tide was pushing there at the edge of his consciousness. All he had to do was find that place where he could sink down and be invisible, untroubled, free of everything. Lost to the night. *Nulli secundus.* Second to none. For his, he believed, was the head that ruled.

Non omnis moriar. Not all of me shall die.

Probably it was the thunder that woke them that night, well before dawn. The heat that had been building for days had finally broken, and because they couldn't go back to sleep Georgina and Jax, separately, went down the back stairs to the kitchen, looking for something to settle them. Expecting to find their mother there. Their mother, whose sleep was so erratic and unpredictable they'd given up trying to understand it and had gotten used to a lifetime of appearances and disappearances. Of finding her on different couches throughout the house in any number of rooms.

She must be asleep, they said when they found the kitchen empty. Surprised that she'd actually done it, gone to bed and stayed.

After a day like today, Georgina said, we should all be dead asleep. And my legs are still killing me from that edging.

The storm was in full rage and rain flew at the windowpanes. Lightning flashes caught the trees mid-shake and they looked alive, threatening, marching on the house, heading for the cliff to topple over it. The light above the stovetop was too soft to obliterate what was beyond the glass, until Georgina switched on the fluorescents overhead and then the only visible world was the kitchen.

Jax cut a big triangle of fruitcake.

She's been making those, Georgina said, putting the kettle on and then cutting her own wedge, all week. Ever since she spoke to Pip about coming over, it's been one cake after another. And I've been eating them—I need to stop.

I'll take a turn, Jax grinned. I'm starving. She stuffed the piece into her mouth.

She always makes these when we're pregnant, Georgina murmured. It's only a shortcut recipe. Not like a *Christmas* cake with all the soaking and stewing and spiking, but still.

Yeah, Jax agreed, even though she had no idea what Georgina was talking about. She'd had two babies and today was the first she'd heard—or tasted—of these cakes. That tour was a bust, wasn't it? she said.

I don't think any of it went to plan.

Jax snorted. Unless the plan was crazy-time. I think those people were out on day passes. Or a field trip. Some kind of horticultural therapy.

Mum seemed pretty upset.

And what about Pippa? She's a mess.

Good thing you're here, Jax, because I couldn't have worked any of that out for myself.

Yeah, you'd be lost without me, eh?

They were quiet then, waiting for the kettle to boil, running through the day's strangeness on their own. Letting the lateness of the hour work on them.

I knew she should've gone to Europe, Jax said finally.

Georgina stared.

Pippa. Aren't we talking about Pippa? If she'd done her gap year bumming around Europe, she wouldn't have met Leo. No kids. Problem solved. I mean, why the fuck would you go to *New Zealand* anyway?

Georgina leaned back against the sink, feeling it was her kitchen now, that she was in charge, the one with experience and authority because hadn't Jax just revealed herself as juvenile?

Just—Georgina snapped her fingers—wish those kids away? That's your solution?

Just my fantasy. Sliding back up onto the counter, dangling her legs, remembering how fun it was to bait her older sister. Don't tell me you've never thought about it.

About Philippa, her gap year, and the family she got out of it? No. Surprisingly.

Wishing your kids away, Jax said. In your case, *kid*. Emphasizing how easy Georgina had it with only one measly child while the rest of us, she implied, are suffocating under the combined weight of them.

I think *you're* out on a day pass.

Maybe I should've gotten on that bus with the other patients. Bunch of circus freaks, eh? Did you see the giant? And in the pool, I'm pretty sure that was a bearded lady.

Georgina smiled then, relaxing, starting to laugh as she put tea bags in the mugs, telling her sister about the woman in the sundress and her reaction to the men taking cuttings. And I think I saw someone squatting, back by the lilacs, she said.

Taking a shit? Jax blurted out, eyes wide. Oh my god. And you should've seen Mum's face when that guy walked into the kitchen. He was a frigging *cyclops*.

Jax pantomimed a look of exaggerated terror and now both sisters were laughing . . . and perhaps it was that, the camaraderie that Pippa sensed, or the storm, or a determined attempt to do something, to put herself in motion, that made her stand up and go downstairs to join her sisters in the kitchen around the island, feeding off cake crumbs, accepting a cup of tea, sliding herself up onto the countertop beside Jax, just as they'd done when they were teenagers and killing time. She didn't talk, but at least she was there—and wasn't that a start? And Jax and Georgina, surprised but hoping that this was a change for the positive, kept gossiping about the day as if she was in on that too. The slapstick chaos of the garden tour, their father galloping through it in his nightclothes, the damage the people had done . . . trying to jolly their little sister along. To make her feel part of something other than whatever was holding her down. They asked her questions but didn't wait for answers, they included her in their observations and analysis of their parents and the row they were heading for, placing themselves and Pippa solidly in that track of kids bitching about how unfair the adult world was to them. Resurrecting that familiar enemy, arraying themselves in formation against it like a corps, reminding her she had a place in the world no matter what.

Eventually, though, their energy flagged, and the sisters all went back to their beds to try to sleep through the remainder of the storm and of the night. Georgina feeling that here, at last, was a change for the better.

Jax stood at the window on the third-floor landing and looked down through the storm to the city spread out below her, its lights insistent, the long ribbons of them leading to where she knew the enormous black smear of Lake Ontario was. At night, that lake was the absence of light. You could trace its edges by the flicker of industry, the shifting headlights, the false dawn of Toronto at the horizon . . . and she thought not about the tour and its eccentricities but about how, when she'd lived here, she'd been beautiful. Young and strong and beautiful. Suitors— she looked at her reflection in the dimpled glass—had come calling in droves. She'd chosen her husband over all of them. But what if he was just another adventure that had simply run its course? What if she'd made a mistake? There was that boy from long ago . . . their memories, what it had felt like to be together . . . she would have said yes if he'd asked her to marry him. Wasn't she certain of that?

One day when we're both married to other people, he'd said to her once, *we'll leave them and be together.*

She'd shrugged it off as immaturity but now, with her hips pressed to the windowsill and only the glass stopping her from falling out, she found herself wondering if it was a premonition. A prophecy. There would have been, she thought, a simplicity to staying put. I might have been happier here. And Toronto . . . a career could flourish there. *Marquees with my name.* So many lights, flickering. So many people. So many lives unravelling. Couldn't she just step on one, on his, the loose thread, and follow it back? Pippa was the obvious and immediate reason why she'd come all the way from Florida, but Billy—Billy Boscoe—was in there too. Why couldn't they pick up where they'd left off? Why shouldn't we? she'd thought, his email boldface on her screen. His message saying that he'd be in town. Twenty years of nothing, and now this.

It's not me, she'd reasoned as she booked her flight out of Florida. Not me who's initiating things. Pure happenstance . . . Her excuses already bleeding out.

Sunday

15

The next day, Jax looked down from her bedroom and marvelled at the lavender drifted up against the boxwood, flickering with bees. Even the morning sunlight was coming down in pretty shafts as though the scene, the garden, was too perfect to do anything but just barely sprinkle it with light, everything glistening from the night's storm, downed leaves dusted about like calling cards. A paradise. Jax found herself longing to be wrapped in it like childhood and those summer days of pleasure. Tree forts she'd built, lakes and oceans she'd swum in, camping trips, lying on hot pavement corralling ants, riding her bike, chips and candy from the convenience store. When it was too hot to sleep she and her sisters used to spread blankets on the grass and sleep outside, no tent, just blankets and pillows underneath the sky, waking in the morning covered with dew, running inside to get breakfast. Perhaps their mother had helped with that—getting blankets, finding pillows, defining their boundaries for the night—but Jax didn't think so. As children they were mostly on their own; children the natural fauna of the household.

She crossed to the other window, the cliff side, and looked down thinking how different from the night before, and how nothing downtown had changed. The waterfront, Georgina told her, had been developed, but from where she stood she couldn't see the bike path or the tramway, the interactive museum or even HMCS *Haida*-the only Tribal-class destroyer left in the world, and now open to the public for tours. The chamber of commerce's answer to the totality of Toronto and its five million attractions. Funny thing about familiar views, Jax thought. Not the particulars you remember but the overall. And there, as always, was the modest business district with its handful of tall buildings, trees and houses emanating out from it, the grid of streets, the enormous sheeting of lake beyond and, beyond that, everything else—escarpment, sky, Toronto and the sprawl that ended in cottages and, eventually, wilderness. Tundra. Frozen north. The Pole. *Still waiting for me. Still lying down at my feet.* The same as it had always been.

Just like me, Jax thought dully, untying her hair, coiling and wrapping it around her finger, making another bun, tying it back in place. Forty-two and no closer to Broadway than I was twenty years ago. And that husband—always encouraging me, never questioning the sense of it, never trying to steer me to something more practical. He's a science teacher, for fuck's sake. Supposedly logical. Why support my drive to be a playwright unless, Jax thought, he doesn't care. If he cared he would've tried to save me from myself. She couldn't even think of a character to compare him to because her knowledge of plays, over the years, had been whittled down to almost nothing. Even at its height it was restricted to the canon—to what was taught at her university in this Dominion of Canada. Nothing too provocative, nothing modern, nothing American. Nothing to rely on and measure yourself against. Nobody becomes a playwright, not really, and of the few who do, why would one be me? He must think there's something sexy about writers. That if I just become one, we'll have sex all the time. Just lie around in a drowsy state of post-coitus, fucking on and off. Isn't that all he's interested in? All we ever talk about, how he never gets enough?

Billy, she thought, would never have let it get to this. As if the outspoken teen she'd known would have matured into an even blunter no-nonsense adult.

Jax ran her thumb over the back of her hand, over the liver spot that had appeared there earlier that summer, and recognized the gesture. It was her mother's. It was what she'd been doing in those quiet moments when Jax came upon her seated in the garden or at the breakfast table before everyone woke up, tracing the patterns of time upon her skin. She was aging, and now so am I. Her husband had seen it first. He'd tapped it with his finger, and smirked.

She lay back on the bed, staring at the sloped ceiling, stretching her legs after her run, and undid the towel she'd wrapped herself in after her shower, letting it fall open and glancing over at the door. Closed but not locked, but then who would trek all the way up to the third floor to discover her there, naked, spread across the bed. She closed her eyes and thought about Billy.

There'd been whispers of that boyfriend ever since she'd arrived without her husband and children; nothing to stop her from listening to them. She tried to remember what they'd done together, how he'd kissed her, what it had felt like to be pressed against his shoulder, the smell of a boy still exhilarating and new, the firmness of his chest. She slid her hand between her legs, remembering his hand beneath the waistband of her panties and how much she'd loved it—the surrender of it, him wanting her, eager but unsure, his fingers finally inside, together, secretive, wherever they could find a place just beyond the party or in the passenger seat of his mother's car. Skirts, she remembered, had made it easier. And camisoles instead of bras.

She moved her hand more quickly, trying to settle on a single image of him, impressions of his back in a faded rugby jersey, his tensed hand resting on the thigh of her jeans, and the harder she tried, the more her mind wandered to other fantasies he wasn't in. She tried forcing him back to the centre of everything, only him, that boy she'd loved and missed, trying to correct the mistake she'd made, but the orgasm she managed barely registered and hardly seemed worth the shower or the towel or the time or any of it. They'd never had sex. Was that the mistake she'd made? There'd been other boys and other sex, but why not with him?

Jax yanked the towel across herself. Idiot, she thought. Maybe it's true, that only my husband has rights to this.

William Boscoe, she said in a whisper. William. Billy. Jacqueline Boscoe. Jax. She said her nickname the way he used to say it, like a snap. The cracking of a whip.

She'd find out soon enough.

———

Georgina, going up to get dressed, met her mother on the stairs.

Darling, Margaret said, pausing on her way down. Have you had your breakfast?

I'm going up.

Your sisters?

Sleeping. Unless Jax is out running, but I don't think so.

Her mother continued past her. And your father? she said, over her shoulder as if he was an afterthought.

Georgina shrugged. Garden, she offered. A guess. But as soon as she said it she was certain it was true—that he'd be out there straightening up and erasing all evidence of that debacle the previous day. Tidying, fixing, ordering and then putting his attention on reframing the entire experience as a tour de force.

I suppose I'll have to make him a cup of tea, Margaret sighed, as though resigned to forever making cups of tea for this husband who was always somewhere else. Would you like one too, Georgie?

Georgina paused at the top of the stairs, arrested by the childish moniker.

Why don't you get Pippa down, Margaret called up to her. See if she'll eat. You can tell her I'm making her a tea, and there's cake.

Margaret hoped that was true, that the one she'd made the day before was still there. More than a mouthful, anyway—more than a few crumbs. I'll have to make another one, she thought briskly, as if everything depended on her and what she could do. She listened to her daughter upstairs walking across to Pippa's bedroom and then, a few seconds later, coming back to the stairs.

She's not there, Georgina called down.

What do you mean?

Pip's not in her room.

Did you check the bathroom?

Georgina shouted that she had.

She's probably—. Margaret hesitated, trying to think of something plausible her daughter might be doing.

I'll look around, Georgina said abruptly. She's probably gone looking for something in another room.

Margaret listened to Georgina's shouts fade to one end of the house, upstairs to the second floor and up again to the third, where Pippa might have wandered for old time's sake, the closets up there still filled with the girls' bric-a-brac. But it was only Georgina who thundered back down again. Standing in the kitchen, she stared blankly at her mother.

She's not up there, Georgina said slowly. But someone else is.

Margaret stared.

A girl. Asleep in one of the beds. I thought it was Jax, but Jax is in her own room getting dressed and this other one has peroxided hair.

Margaret stared at her daughter, still failing to comprehend, still focused on Pippa because it was inconceivable that the daughter she'd seen off to sleep the night before, so newly arrived from New Zealand and a wreck, could have gone anywhere by herself.

But . . . where's Philippa?

Maybe she went for a walk, Georgina suggested. Maybe Dad's taking her around the garden.

The garden?

Georgina left her mother then. Left her standing at her place by the kettle, still in her nightdress and dressing gown, automatically dunking tea bags and pouring milk and spooning and stirring the sugar in, while she went outside to search the garden. The only one, her impatience said, with any sense.

Margaret stayed inside, drifting from window to window, looking out, following Georgina's shouts, becoming more and more worried as the shouts went unanswered, trying to calm herself by remembering that Pippa was hardly in a condition to shout back. They'd have to stumble upon her to find her. Where would she want to be? Margaret didn't know. When her children had gone outside she'd never followed them, she just let them go, glad for the distance it created and the peace and quiet. A chance for her to work. Pippa would have a favourite place, Margaret was sure of that, but it would be a secret and they'd have to discover it for themselves. Her husband was looking now too. She could see him stalking between the beds, one hand still gripping a tool, and she hated him then. As if everything was his fault. As if last night had driven their daughter out. And when Georgina and David came down the drive together empty-handed to the house, she had to steady herself against the kitchen counter.

The cliff, she wanted to shout at them. Go and check the cliff.

But when she said it her voice was small as though even the suggestion that Pippa was capable of that was a blow to her. It took her saying it a second time to make them go and look. It took her threatening to go and look herself.

She watched them move out across the escarpment, lean over the fence, look down. Suicide, she knew, was possible. She had tried it once herself.

And what, she thought vaguely, had Georgina meant about another girl upstairs?

Margaret climbed the stairs to the third floor, pausing frequently to catch her breath, to delay the inevitable, and when it came—when she pushed the door open and saw the girl from the garden tour lying there—it knocked her lower than her knees.

She backed out, locked the door and pocketed the key.

This was David's doing, she was sure of it. He must have put her there.

16

Margaret took the stairs slowly on the way back down. It was a long time since she'd been all the way up to the third floor. The pretty floral wallpaper she'd chosen when they'd moved in was torn now in jagged sections and the plaster beneath it, unpainted, looked faintly mildewed. Her children would have done this—grabbing the unfurling corners and riding the paper sheets down like a zipline—the animals. The bannister under her hand was sticky with dirt and dug out in places, as if someone had struck at it randomly with a hatchet. Multiple outbursts of teenage anger, she supposed. Thankful again that this house was so big its empty spaces had absorbed much of that. It had been easy, in a house this size, to avoid confrontations and she realized now, seeing the evidence, that the fights she'd had with her children only represented a fraction of their anger and she was glad the house had borne the brunt of that.

Goldilocks.

Margaret named the girl she'd locked in that room receding behind her, trying to recast the key in the pocket of her dressing gown as something foretold and inevitable—part of a well-worn narrative that would play out along the expected tracks those stories follow where she—Goldilocks—was nothing more than a device. A fairy tale. Not a person whom Margaret had just imprisoned without having any kind of plan in mind. Without considering the consequences, or even really meaning to—just driven by an impulse to freeze things as they were until she could make sense of them. Perhaps there was a lesson there, but Margaret had chosen not to read it that way and by the time she reached the second-floor landing she'd put Goldilocks far down the list of what was important, because her baby was still out in the world somewhere, with no one to look after her, and Margaret knew that *that* was where the real danger lay. In moving beyond the confines and security of this house and family.

She could hear them, her husband and one of her daughters, down below in the kitchen, and as soon as she laid eyes on David his efforts of the night before came booming back and Margaret saw immediately, in his swagger, that he was revelling in them. Cock-of-his-walk, preening himself before this world laid low in front of his magnificence. And now that she knew about the girl upstairs, his strut was almost unbearable. The key in her pocket became, in that instant, a dagger she would thrust at him. Small and neat, she'd just barely pierce his jugular to make him hemorrhage in misty spurts and then she'd step back and watch as he clamped an ineffectual hand across the puncture. She would make him bleed out, right in front of her. Margaret slid her hand around the key as she entered the kitchen, keeping it there because just knowing she had it was enough for now. She waited for someone else to speak first because they were all there now—even Jax, roused from her bed and already in her bathing suit. But they were all looking to her.

So, she said finally into the silence. So? Go and search the neighbourhood.

Jax went back upstairs to get dressed, and David and Georgina walked along the lane as they'd been told to. Neither was talking because what was there to talk about. It was clear that the tour had been an absolute disaster and if either of them were able to think laterally, they'd see it correctly as the precipitous event that had put them in the shitstorm they were in now—dodging potholes and looking for a missing person they both knew they wouldn't find. Not like this.

Bloody cheapskates, David growled as he skirted the craters, waving an arm at the house on his right. Look at them with their fancy cars . . . Audis, Mercedes, Land Rovers, a Rolls-Royce with right-hand drive . . . The potholes, he exploded into his daughter's silence. The *ruddy* potholes.

The entire lane was his property, deeded with the house, and the lane's other residents had right-of-way. Legally, repairs were his responsibility, but David didn't think it was fair that he should have to pay for everything when all the residents were making use of and degrading it. It wasn't cheap to maintain a road. So he'd worked out a formula, a sliding scale based on use so that he—at the lane's end—paid the most, and the person in the first house paid the least. It was, he felt, an equitable share of the cost. He'd worked it out in great detail before calling a meeting to present it to the other residents, but he'd seen the way their eyes had cased his living room and all its treasures, and once the meeting was over, and they weren't face to face anymore, the other two houses had refused to pay anything for maintenance or improvements. Every few years he tried again and still they refused, so every spring the snow melted to reveal deeper and deeper holes as he let the surface deteriorate to teach them a lesson. Never mind, as his wife liked to point out, that it is really *we* at the end who are suffering the most.

Georgina nodded, pressing her lips together in a manner she hoped looked like sympathy. She knew his anger was building again and she just wanted to delay it until she was clear because she, like her mother, was alarmed by the bombshell of Pippa's disappearance and she needed to concentrate on working out how to get her back, not on answering her father's tantrums which were tiresome and far too regular and, this time, grossly inopportune.

They fell into step with each other as if they were just out for a stroll and catching up on news: the little threads that bind families together. A father and his adult daughter, chatting . . . a rich man with his pretty young thing. So everyday, so innocuous, that anyone would think them bright and clean and free of trouble. Would be envious that they could afford the luxury of a mid-morning constitutional, an airing out, a prescription of moderate exercise . . . But as they walked, the roar of the traffic up the escarpment was becoming louder and more insistent. Pippa was out there somewhere in all that hustle, and they were meant to be finding her.

You go that way, David said when they arrived at the lane's end, and he turned to walk in the other direction—out into the capillaries and veins and arteries of the monstrous city that surrounded them. Out to do battle, to repossess one of his own. And Georgina, surprised by his forcefulness, didn't argue. And it didn't matter, because neither of them really believed they'd find Pippa wandering the neighboring streets. They were just doing what they'd been told, and as quickly as possible, so they could get back to the house again, which was where the answer was sure to present itself.

In truth, David thought his wife was overreacting about Philippa, but after last night there was a logic to maintaining the peace. He didn't fear being overthrown, he was secure in his position, but he did want to enjoy the afterburn of the sex they'd had because it didn't come around often enough. Not like that. He needed to soak in it. And there'd been the additional windfall of that girl having performed for him outside . . . and the thrilling fact it had been his wife who'd shown him to the front-row seat. That, perhaps, was the most delicious part of all of this. His wife—her vulgarity laid bare. She'd wanted it just as badly as him, and instead of draining the excitement from his conquest it had made it even more pleasurable. A promise of more, much more, to come. She'd always taken whatever he'd delivered, but now she'd opened up the possibilities into realms he'd never thought she'd let him conquer. Other women? And why shouldn't he. David stopped and did a deep knee bend, rising suddenly. *More vigorous than men half my age.*

That garden tour, he thought smugly, was the catalyst for all of this. He quickened his step. *A job exceedingly well done.*

—

It felt strange at first, walking without a particular destination, just meandering, but after a few blocks David forgot about that and started paying attention to the houses and their gardens and, just as he'd expected, most of them were horrible. No gardens at all. Just threadbare plots of what he supposed the owners called grass, and smack in the middle of every front yard was a tree. Maples mostly, every tenth one a birch. There was obviously a formula to it, some sort of rationale worked out by the city's arborist or determined by the budget, or simply put there to insist on the Canadian identity. To scream MAPLE LEAF! the way the national flag did. Of all the trees they could have chosen. David was a champion of exotics, of flowering, blossoming extravagance, because what was life without excess. Although, he admitted, the maples were lovely when they turned. He had three or four himself. But to have them—infinitum—in a row down the street like lampposts . . .

These houses were all small red brick boxes with little concrete pads jutting out from their front doors, basement windows peeking apologetically from the ground and sealed driveways marking the boundary between the next red box of a house, and so on and so on. Like a Monopoly board except that people actually lived in them, tiny as they were. Every now and then the window next to the front door would be puffed out into a bay, like a swelling.

Fifty of these would fit into mine, he thought.

But it was not so much that which he objected to—the meagreness of them—as it was the occupants' acceptance of it. Yes, it was a small patch, but something could still be done with it.

Why did they settle for such modesty? There was no hint of ambition anywhere.

He stopped for a moment. Someone had made an effort here. There were common hydrangea bushes under the bay window and they went from pink at one end to a puzzling blue at the other. How had they done that, made the soil change so drastically? Made the roots draw their nutrients so selectively? He had to walk across the lawn and right up to them before he noticed they were planted in pots that had been sunk into the ground, realizing the deception. Well, he thought. Here's a surprise. Clumsy but effective, and it had fooled him from a distance. If they'd been planted in the ground the colours would be uniform—aesthetically more pleasing, but disappointingly uniform. By sinking them in pots, each one with a different ratio of aluminum to soil, whoever had planted them had created an above-ground colour graph of differing composition like a botanical diagram. He felt heartened by that. Buoyed. Not a patch on his display, of course, but in this house at least someone was thinking, showing some initiative. One bright spot after blocks and blocks of mindless repetition.

He glanced up at the house, through the window, his chin just at the windowsill. Nothing special, as far as he could see. Couch, chair, rug, corner of a table, a few poorly framed photographs on the wall and in the back, where a light was on, the small kitchen. He could make out a white refrigerator jutting a few inches into the open doorway, its coils exposed. It was everything he would have expected if he'd ever thought about it, which he hadn't.

Still, he thought, stepping back, taking the hydrangeas in again. Well done. Well done, indeed.

He carried on, his tempo up, even though he knew the hydrangeas were meagre and their pots were plastic, probably with their cheap prices still stickered to their sides. But even so . . . it was something. An attempt. Because life—he flicked at a leaf as he walked—is best when it's directed, controlled, bent to a vision of how it ought to be. Perhaps—he slowed, the thought coming to him now—perhaps I've somewhat failed at that, and he remembered Philippa and why he was here. I should have pruned those girls. Fed them more selectively. He looked around himself, at the conventional neighbourhood, which collared his majestic house-and-five-acres, with its uniform streets and repeating curb-cuts and its mundane tracery of wires bringing electricity to the people who lived there. And for what? To run their freezers and their televisions, to heat and cool their houses while they were away at work—to keep the dull hum of their lives powered on. *Have I raised my girls only to transplant them into this?* It was like an explosion at his feet, the idea that he'd produced something that might slide into mediocrity.

Margaret pulled their bedsheets tight, smoothed the duvet, spread flat the enormous jewel-red silk fabric she'd bought in India, so sumptuous she'd bought it even though she didn't need it. Curtains, she'd thought vaguely at the time. Cushion covers? It didn't matter so long as it was hers. She liked collecting things whose utility was outdone by their pure luxury because what was a life if it wasn't rife with beauty—and how else to smother all the filth that was always there and threatening to take over. Which had been, if she was honest, her reaction to India as a whole.

She was trying to gather the strength to pull the curtains back, raise the blinds and let the pale sunlight in. For now, for another minute, it was enough just to stand there as if the day hadn't started and the house was as she'd left it the night before, with everyone in bed, the storm just beginning, and her children snug—without Pippa gone missing. Without her husband taking everything out on her. Without that girl upstairs.

Margaret scraped the heavy curtains across their rails and pulled the blinds up. It was wet. Dew was holding the petals down and making leaves droop, and each blade of grass, as the weak sunbeams hit them, looked beaten. The night's storm had deadheaded and torn blooms off their stems, and a branch from the hawthorn tree had been downed across the lily bed. She could see the end of it poking out onto the grass like the barrel of a sniper's gun. It had been years since she'd been out there and worked that soil, her joints giving her trouble and too painful now, most of the time, to bend and lift and carry. And as the years had accumulated, as if the garden itself was turning on her, insect bites and even glancing contact with the plants had become fully blown allergic reactions that antihistamines couldn't treat. Even prednisone didn't always work, and on the last few occasions that she'd been stricken it was only an injection of epinephrine that had done the trick. David, she thought, had taken some pleasure in that—administering it with what she thought was an unnecessary vigour that had left her bruised.

She missed the simple work of raising plants. The way you could tear them out when they failed and replace them with newer, stronger variants. Disappointments, in the garden, were so easily remedied. Upon his semi-retirement, David had fired their gardening help and taken to gardening himself. Actual gardening, not just the plotting out of beds on bits of paper as he'd always done before, but really pulling weeds and pruning bushes and thinning and dividing, his hands scratched and his knees pitted and dirty. She tried not to let it bother her the way he talked about it as if he was the only one who knew what it was like to plant twenty rose bushes in a single morning, or edge five beds or trim all the yews bordering the terrace. He liked to stand in the kitchen, with a cup of tea in one hand and a hastily made sandwich in the other, and list everything he'd done and everything he had still to do—the reason he couldn't sit and rest like her. The reason his lunch was makeshift. The reason he'd drink his tea regardless, even though she'd over-sugared it or made it too strong or too weak or too milky. All the ways, he implied, you try to sabotage me. And all the ways I carry on. *Pede poena claudo*. Punishment comes limping. Even before he'd reduced his office days down to three a week (and now two), David had always meddled—the initial strike being the time he'd dug up her potager garden.

It had happened on a rare Saturday when she'd gone in to Toronto with an old art school friend, to see the Picasso Exhibition: Blue Period. Margaret remembered that because she and her friend had talked about how oddly specific that was, to curate only those few years, but also how that quirk made the show doable in one afternoon. They'd stayed in town for dinner and by the time Margaret arrived home it was dark, and all the evidence of David's trespass was invisible. It wasn't until she went out to the porch the next morning that she saw the swathe of humped dirt where only the previous morning there'd been cucumbers, zucchini, beans and an entire crop of other edibles. Neat groupings that she'd clipped and trimmed and shifted and replaced until every sightline revealed something startling and beautiful; a pure extravagance of a vegetable garden that produced enough food to feed the neighbourhood if they'd been so inclined.

An orangery, he'd said simply when she'd turned on him. *Obviously.* Smaller than I'd like, but when I'm finished it will be an exact replica of the one Queen Anne built at Kensington Palace. In *1704*, he'd added, to underscore how much more enduring it would be than her merely seasonal vegetables that needed harvesting and replanting year after year. The workmen, he informed her, start tomorrow.

David, with that one blow, had ruined this tiny corner of the garden for her and shown how quickly he'd move in when given the chance, bulldozing and imprinting it with ready-made plans that came steeped in precedent. How swiftly he would undo her decades of sculpting by intuition in order to impose his false pedigrees.

He'd made it easy for her to give up. To retreat, to stop noticing.

Pippa, Margaret thought, staring now at the windowsill, has to be all right. She refused to believe otherwise. Whatever it took, she'd get her back. She wouldn't lose another one.

When Georgina saw her father, he was standing on the grassy verge but making no move to step down to the road and cross, or back onto the sidewalk. He looked helpless and old. Vacant. His dirty clothes were torn in places and his hair was dishevelled as though it were windy. As though he were lost high on a mountaintop, like a hermit who'd just left his cave and to whom the larger world was bewildering. She felt sorry for him then, knowing how much he'd wanted everything to go perfectly and how disappointed he must be that it hadn't—that his garden had been desecrated, because she knew how deeply he felt about it. That to him it was more than a grouping of plants, or a division of plots—it was a final destination, a mecca, a heavenly sphere with the house at its centre. And right now, she thought, he looks just like the sort of beggar who might spin such a tale and believe it too.

We need to call the hospitals, Georgina said. And of course she was right. It didn't take a leap to imagine that Philippa, eight months pregnant, had gone into labour and been taken away from wherever it was she'd gone. Come on, Dad. She took his arm as if he needed steadying, or a caretaker to guide him through this disorienting maze of streets to his leafy country lane. And—Georgina hesitated—we should call the police as well.

But her father wasn't listening. She knew this pose; the studied look.

I thought it went well, she said, softening her tone. The tour, I mean.

Her choice was simple: she could tell him that none of it, not *any* of it—all his weeks of work and preparation—had been worth a jot, or she could just play along with what she knew would be a rapid trajectory from letdown to victory, because he always turned his errors into achievements he could boast about. And now that he was old and—she looked at him beside her, frail—there was something sweet and winning about that. An affectation she'd disliked when she was younger but now seemed harmless or, at worst, eccentric.

When Jax met them at the gateposts, only now dressed and

ready to help, it was David who told her what the plan was—hospital and police—as if he'd come up with it himself. Assuming control.

But—, Jax said slowly as if she was just now beginning to piece things together. Just now waking up. Are you sure Pip's not upstairs? I'm sure I heard someone up there this morning—down the other end of the attic—

There was someone, Georgina said, but not Pippa. A girl. Platinum hair.

Their father didn't hear them. He was already striding ahead, neatly back inside his conviction that his were the only thoughts that mattered. And so he missed it. Missed the news that would have set him to galloping.

Mum said it must be a friend of Pippa's, Georgina said. Remember that hippie commune phase she had? Probably one of them. They're always looking for a place to crash, and must've heard that Pip was back. Mum said she'd take care of it. Get her out.

This, Jax sighed, looking around at nothing in particular but including all of it, has been a royally fucked-up handful of days . . . And she hadn't even seen Billy yet.

17

The night before, during the storm, Pippa hadn't gone back to bed like her sisters had. She'd gone up the back stairs with them but then quietly, stealthily, she'd come down the front stairs and around to the kitchen, slid into Jax's flip-flops and gone outside and begun to walk. Down the driveway, the lane and, on a whim, the overgrown trail leading to the busy access road below the house. Walking steadily like that nun from thirty years ago, ignoring the sudden claps of thunder, driven, automatic. How many years had it been since she'd taken this route? She'd remembered it gradually, step by step, down the lane and through the trees to the road's edge, teetering a moment on the curb before sprinting the six lanes to get across and then the mad energy of the storm became hers and she forgot the baby she was carrying and raised her face to the rain to feel it, the storm. Crying, laughing, hysterical, she could really feel it now.

There was the trail she used to ride her bike down, shorts and tank top, strong and fit. There were the old wooden stairs, straight down and precipitous. *Not the stairs*, she'd thought, turning into the dark of the trail, needing something more gradual and intimate, something to hold her close. She'd needed coddling, even as she charged ahead. She had slowed then. It was sheltered from the rain under the trees but dark, and the trail wasn't as solid as she'd remembered it. More like a gully of loose gravel than a trail. She'd pushed on anyway, through the lightning flashes and down the long, lazy switchbacks she used to ride her bike down, remembering the thrill and exhilaration of barely escaping injury as her tires pounded against rocks, the back wheel fishtailing and the handlebars reverberating with shocks carrying right up through her arms to her head. Once upon a time she'd used this route so regularly she could anticipate every turn and bump and every break in the tree canopy where the sun would shoot through and blind her for a moment before releasing her to the shadows again. This trail had connected her with the city. With her friends and downtown and her part-time jobs. There'd been the summer she'd lifeguarded at the yacht club's pool, even though her only qualification was being able to swim, and she'd ridden her bike back and forth each day and become tanned and as taut as an athlete, which was something she and her sisters had never been mistaken for. Even Jax, who'd been on teams, had never been very good at any of the sports—but her "spirit," one coach had told her, more than made up for that.

It had felt good to be walking outside, where no one could see or bother her. Where she could do as she pleased as though nothing at all was the matter. As though what stretched before her and what was littered behind her were the same—possibility—without the hard lump of inertia her life had become. When she'd been pregnant with her first, she remembered, there'd been dancing. She and a group of women—first-time mothers, all of them—would meet at each other's houses, send the men away and turn the stereo up as loud as it would go. They'd switch the lights off and let the music spin them, move them, hold them . . . it wasn't exercise so much as it was freedom. They'd drop their clothes and just move with the music, on and on, until one by one when they'd had enough, they would get dressed and go home. All their senses jangling. It had been a spontaneous gathering at first, and then gradually became organized as they drew up a roster of whose house they'd meet at next.

As their babies were born they stopped dancing and started nursing and sharing strategies, and it became just another place where schedule was paramount. With more children it became a playdate, and soon they were all too busy to meet and any dancing was in the grocery aisle between the cart and the children and the frozen foods. They started using preprinted shopping lists because nothing ever changed—they would always need two packets of noodles and a frozen pizza, week after week after week. And it was the women now, not the men, who longed to be sent away, because as much as Pippa tried to make parenting into something that functioned on the level of salvation—raising perfection to inherit the earth, saving the planet one child at a time, modelling peace and love and happiness, ending hunger, redefining poverty, being kind to animals, letting boys wear sparkles and girls dress up as pirate men—it wasn't. It was none of that at all. It was bribery and corruption, it was waste and all-out war. It was her forever marshalling them into something society would accept. It was giving in and selling out.

She'd tried conjuring her four little boys but she couldn't get more than a scratch. The feeling of being raked over with finger-nails. Was that really how she thought of them? Tiny clutching grasping grabby little hands? Soundless and cruel? It wasn't the family she'd set out to make. Where had the bright wooden toys and the homemade play-dough and the piles and piles of pic-ture books gone? Those boys had eaten nothing but breast milk and natural food served on dishes of real porcelain. It had been a continuous twenty-four-hour cycle of loving and hugging and nocturnal shifts into their parents' bed until by morning the whole family was draped across each other like a heap of laun-dry, their bedroom a den. She'd set out to construct a utopia of wonder and amazement, populated by little foot soldiers of joy who would go out into the world and cast that joy around—a storybook on homemade paper, written in vegetable dyes and drawn with love, where the words were symbols so anyone could understand . . . But what she'd gotten were junkyard dogs. Scrappy animals. A howling mess.

And Leo. Leo, her husband, was having sex with other women. It had begun as an arrangement to benefit them both— she'd take the husband and he'd take the wife—but it wasn't what she'd bargained for at all. And certainly not this pregnancy from out of that jumble of multiple partners. If she could only walk far enough, she'd thought, and hard enough, she could leave it all behind. This rain might scour and cleanse her and when day broke, she'd be as remade as the land.

Pippa had woken in the lee of the escarpment that Sunday morning, wedged between the two massive chunks of limestone she'd retreated to when the storm had become too powerful to face. When the thunder and lightning collapsed together and the rain had become as thick and cold as driving snow. It hadn't been dry where she'd taken refuge, but it had been out of the wind and secure enough that she'd fallen asleep, waking now to the battered silence of morning. She didn't move, just sat there propped up against the rocks, legs splayed in front of her, one of her hands raking the dirt between her legs, tiny sticks jamming under her fingernails. And her baby, as if to show how resilient it was and how different from this mother who couldn't bring herself to do anything worthwhile, was writhing and turning like a rock hurtling downhill. As if it was trying to wake its host body and get it back on track to survival.

Where was she? Trees all around. Pippa squinted but couldn't see a single house through the layers of trunks and branches and leaves, squirrels and birds skittering through the storm's destruction. They're looting, she thought. Scavenging. Cleaning up. Some kind of moral in there, she guessed, but she didn't care to make the leap. She was tired of making connections, threading things along as if life was just a craft to keep your fingers occupied. It had to be more than that. More than a cobbling-together. More than a giant spillway of happenstance. More than a blind stumble from thing to thing with no reflection, no looking back or forward, no over-arching plan. Didn't there have to be more to life than drift?

Staring in front of her, she thought how different this was and how she would have never been able to see through New Zealand woods like she could see through these ones. Never identify individual trunks, the sunbeams cutting through, birds swooping like fish through this air liquid with drafts. And butterflies, scores of butterflies. New Zealand was beautiful but it wasn't this. It was native bush, feathery with ferns and lush with pongas and flax. It was a downy muted softness. Was that what was wrong with her? Was it only a question of coming home for good? Laying herself and her life across a particular landscape . . . that the land itself was what would fix her? For a while, last night, before the storm drove her to shelter, she'd thought there'd been an improvement under way, but now she knew it had just been the adrenalin of risk. Her world, in New Zealand, was just repetition and routine. The jolt of the unfamiliar, the bristle of danger that had put her out there in the storm—it didn't happen down there. Even the sex with other couples had become ordinary, in its way. She supposed she'd always thought that one day she'd keep going and complete her circumnavigation of the globe. That the family she'd made over there would come home here too. But how could Leo trade the Pacific Ocean for Lake Ontario? Trade a lifetime of being on the ocean for a landlocked freshwater basin that was frozen half the year? And how had she never even considered that?

Pippa smoothed the dirt and then raked it back again. There were ants, but not the biting kind, and she let them run over her, brushing them lightly if they got too high—as if that absent-minded motion wasn't maiming them. When they were kids, she and her sisters, they used to set them on fire by angling a magnifying glass and concentrating the sun on their tiny bodies, making them combustible, because they were just ants and therefore numberless and impossible to decimate. In New Zealand, her children pulled the tails off lizards or hung them from their ears, tiny reptilian jaws snapping shut on their fleshy lobes. Earrings, they'd giggle on the playground, shaking their heads at their friends. Every place, Pippa supposed, has its petty cruelties. Every childhood its atrocities.

And hadn't she had her share of those?

It was Leo who'd suggested it, and it hadn't seemed a stretch. He was generous with everyone. His fishing charter that day, he'd told her over the dishes, had been swingers.

We smoked a few joints, and it got pretty hot. I mean, watching them.

They had *sex* on the boat? And you watched?

No, he laughed, tapping her nose with his finger. Just messing around. Kissing and stuff.

He cupped her breast. Ran his hand under the curve of it and down. Tucked his fingers in the waistband of her shorts.

She'd laughed. He couldn't be serious. Nobody did that anymore. It wasn't the first time he'd mentioned someone else but it had always been in the middle of sex when a lot of things were said and never followed through with. Never after dinner, when they were cleaning the kitchen and the boys were in the next room watching television.

There's a service, he said. It's anonymous. They set you up.

It had started like that. A bit of news from his day. A suggestion, a dare—and in the end she'd taken it because it seemed to fit with all the other decisions she'd made, which weren't decisions at all but simple reactions to whatever came in front of her. And weren't they finished having kids? And hadn't they earned some fun for themselves? *We had*—he reminded her—*ten years before the babies started coming*. Wasn't it time to go back to that?

Yeah, okay, she'd said a week later. Giving in. Why not.

But he enjoyed it more than she did. Especially when she got pregnant this time. She stopped altogether when the pregnancy advanced and even though he said he'd stop too, she knew he hadn't. Knew that too often his errands were invented and that now it was Leo and the husbands, both sharing the wife. And that left her . . . where? And safe sex, in the context of swinging, had seemed counterintuitive and oxymoronic. The other husbands all said they'd had vasectomies, but the scars were too microscopic to see, so how could she be sure? And vasectomies, like anything, can fail. Marriage, she'd thought recklessly at the time, is its own sort of birth control. Bastard-proof, anyway. But now that she was pregnant, she realized she didn't know for certain who the father was.

Pippa rolled onto her knees, walking her hands up the opposing boulders until she was standing, letting the weight of her baby settle. She had to get away from here. I should've had a plan, she thought. All along, I should've had a plan. Life had just carried her—and what did that make her? A peddler of truths so hackneyed and shallow she couldn't even form the words now without all the moisture evaporating from her mouth. Without her mouth clacking like a castanet: No television. No sugar. No polyester, BPAs, generic sunblock or corporate mosquito repellent. No saying no. With the other mothers, she'd squatted on the grass unwrapping cotton napkins filled with homemade granola bars and nuts and fruit and let the children circle in to graze whenever they wanted to, their whims and impulses paramount. She'd swapped platitudes. She'd wept for the children with their babysitters who were never allowed to go barefoot or shirtless or without a hat in the summertime, and who stuck to a schedule that never changed. Who were secured in a swing and pushed for an hour, and then strapped to a stroller and escorted home for a nap even if they were five years old and had done nothing to tire themselves out. Probably given cough syrup or valerian root in their lunch to make them sleep.

We're better, Pippa and her mothers agreed. We're down here at the level of our child, taking our cues from them, our only preconceived ideas that what is natural and spontaneous is always best. And how can that possibly hurt anyone?

But when they grow, Pippa thought now, they leave you down there on the ground. At least Pippa had been left. The other mothers had gone back to work—shedding the granola like a summer tan—whereas Pippa was down there still, her children clambering across her as if she were a jungle gym, their droppings in her hair. All those babies had been her way of fixing the rut she'd fallen into when life with Leo had become just life, no longer the excitement and adventure and novelty it had started out as. She'd thought babies could fix anything. But she was an adult and adults, Pippa thought in her lucid moments, are supposed to have a plan. Long-term, not just day-to-day. Why had her parents never taught her that? Insisted on it. Realized she was flailing, and reeled her in? At *least* made her go to university and get a degree, some sort of basic credentials. Why hadn't they objected more strenuously to her sudden marriage?

Her husband had looked relieved when she'd told him she was going home for a rest. Leo's answer to her problem was to smoke more weed and leave joints for her on the nightstand or in the bathroom so there was always one handy if she wanted it. He busied himself with the cooking and the chores, taking the older boys to work on the boat with him and dropping the younger two off at the Maori neighbours up the street who had so many kids of their own a few more wouldn't make a difference. She doubted he'd even cleared it with them first. *He'll be glad I've gone away.* It would make it easier for him, her not being there to bring him down. He wouldn't have to try and understand why she couldn't just snap out of it—be pregnant, have a baby, and get on with it like she'd done every other time. Why she had to make such a fuss. He could go back to enjoying things.

When the trail began to climb again, away from the fences and yards, Pippa started to seriously doubt her course. And when, through a gap in the trees, she saw the tall spire of the cathedral, which she knew was near the highway at the city's western edge, she knew she'd come too far. She was nowhere near downtown or the neighbourhood where all her friends lived: she'd somehow missed everything, and was out where the city bled into wilderness.

She couldn't get anything right, not even escape. Pippa sat down, defeated. There hadn't been a single other person on that trail and she knew why, swatting the mosquitoes the storm had loosed. It was humid and muggy and if you had any sort of choice where to go, this trail in these woods wouldn't have a shot. Dirt had worked its way into her underwear and it rubbed uncomfortably, and she smelled and had wet herself with the effort of sitting down, everything sticky and grimy and beginning to itch. She lay back. Another minute. Another minute, just to catch her breath, and she'd get up and start walking back the way she'd come. Another minute, she told herself, and she'd be okay. Lying on her back like that, the weight of the baby made it hard to breathe. She turned onto her side, hip grinding against rock, and it was when she pulled her arm up across her chest that the first contraction hit and then there was nothing else but the pain. And why bother with a hospital, she thought wildly, these woods can absorb it just as well. Better, even, no one to hear me scream. She waited, letting the contractions pin her, waiting for her water to break, knowing the baby would be quick like the others had been, that there was no stopping it, ready to get it over with. To get the whole fucking thing over with. And how perfect to be there like an animal, writhing in the dirt. It was what life had brought her to. It was where she belonged. Down on that ground again and no way back up. And she'd done it to herself. Hadn't she done it to herself? The old memory blazing forward like a meteor.

Get on, you little bitch.

All he'd said to her. A growl.

And she'd done it. Drawn the crotch of her bathing suit aside and put his hard dick in with her own hands, her breasts already out, the water slapping them. Legs around to his back like a horsey-ride. Obedient. Forbidden. Because wasn't this what she'd been looking for in every flaming Sambuca, spliff or binge, every line of shooters, every party, every pack of cigarettes smoked down in grotty apartments, every phalanx breached to grab whatever was on the bar, didn't matter, as long as it pushed her further. Why wouldn't she get on? She was eighteen; he wasn't her first.

He was her parents' friend. A friend of their family since before she was born. In every way possible, he was safe. It happened at his cottage one holiday, swimming in the lake with the stars like radioactive crumbs above them, darkness, a frisson of danger like electricity, like the air before a charge, the whole lake pushing them closer until they were waist deep and he was already naked. Waiting. That first time, it was quick. Exhilarating and quick. But each time after that, their sessions went longer and became more complex and he made her do things he said all men would want from her.

I'm schooling you, he'd say as he teased and played with her. Show me how grateful you can be. Making her grovel and perform.

18

There were no special craft tables in the room where Margaret worked above the kitchen, next door to where Pippa should have been sleeping and directly below Goldilocks. It was just an extra room with some bonus furniture and a big oak desk pushed against one wall that might have even been there when they'd bought the house, no one could remember. One window looked out onto the driveway and the other one to the neighbour's property which, at that point, was a dense line of evergreens so substantial they were like the edge of a forest that might continue for miles. In the summer the room was hot, positioned as it was to miss the breezes coming up off the lake. It was a room that nobody wanted. A blind spot in the household's array.

Margaret kept her books in the closet, jammed up on the shelf above the clothes rail. So many, and so big, that the wood sagged under the weight of them. The materials she used to build her collages were collected in messy piles and stacks and bins—just something someone had cleared away from somewhere else and put there, on that side table or in that corner or on a chair or windowsill, because this was the waiting room for things whose fate was unclear. To the rest of the family this was not a studio but a junk room. A wasting place.

She began with the leftover stickers she'd been placing on objects throughout the house. Onto the new pillowcase-sized blank sheet she pulled out, she wrote the date at the top in minuscule numbers only she would know to look for and then placed one round sticker of each colour, for each girl, at the centre. Making them overlap. She didn't need a letter to tell them apart—*she* only needed colours. Everything would radiate from that. Around those stickers now she laid the buds of cotton swabs, snapped off and dipped into glue and held to the page with a carefully placed rotation of flower stems and toothpicks cased in foil, sprays of tinsel that she'd found behind a tin of baked beans in the pantry, a ribbon of red electrical tape securing the brittle spokes of what she now saw was a wheel. Misshapen, it was true, but close enough to being round that it would be able to move, albeit with a clatter. Anyone would hear it coming, even the preoccupied. From the pocket of her dressing gown Margaret pulled out the petals she'd saved from Georgina's bouquets and dusted them behind the wheel like multicoloured gravel kicked up by the screeching velocity of this vehicle she seemed to be constructing. Tiny streaks of pollen marked the paper. She laid clear tape over the bits of flowers as if the tape was the gusting wind, locking everything to the page.

But, no, it's not all flowers, she thought, standing back. Not only sunshine and light. Philippa was gone. She walked around the room, fingering the piles, flicking through bins of castoffs, picking things up, aware of Goldilocks above her—the key heavy in her pocket. She touched a butter knife—its bone handle split, the cap for a bottle of cider, an old Christmas card with a dove on it, rubber letters and numbers from a stamping kit, a length of yarn . . . It wasn't a wheel, she saw now when she circled back and looked at the paper. Not something for transport. It was an eye, the centre of a hurricane, a whirlpool drawing the whole world in and Margaret could feel herself beginning to spin, having tried so hard all morning to act like there was no pain when in fact it hurt to stand or to sit, and even the featherlight satin of her dressing gown chafed her skin. He'd left bruises everywhere. The sore spots on her calves, where his knees had ground into her like pestles, were what tipped her forward now against the desk, and just as she hit the edge, she heard a thud overhead.

Jax was sunbathing, and David and Georgina had gone to the police station to file the missing person report, so when Goldilocks started hammering on the locked door with her fists and screaming obscenities and hurling threats, it was only Margaret—perfectly still at the foot of the attic stairs now—who could hear her.

The voice was more robust than Margaret had imagined it would be. Not deep, like a man's—it was fully feminine, there was no doubting that—but coarse, like a muddied torrent chock full of sticks and stones.

. . . *thisgoddamnedfuckingbullshitcuntrippingmotherfuckerofa* . . .

Margaret held her breath and listened to the vile tattoo beating out. So much rage, she thought simply, taking her first step up.

. . . *bettermotherfuckingopenthismotherfuckingdoororI'llpullyourfucking ballsupthroughyourmouthandfuckingchokeyouwiththemwhenI* . . .

Margaret couldn't help herself. She was hooked by that stream of profanities, pulling her one step at a time, closer and closer, to where the door frame was rattling with all the panic of a bird trapped against a window. She knew it must be hot in there. The windows were painted shut, there'd be no hope of a breeze, and at this time of day the sun would be lighting up the whole room, making it a furnace. She could see the girl's feet backlit at the bottom of the door, in the tiny sliver of space there, and she knew by how they flickered that the girl was jumping. Throwing her whole body against the door trying to break it down. But these doors swung in and were old and heavy, solid wood, and that girl—because Margaret had seen her—was just a chip of a thing. She wouldn't last. She'd give up, pass out, turn to crying or pleading—she didn't have what it took to tear a door right off its hinges. To endure a lifetime of what Margaret had endured.

Margaret sat down and waited. Waited on the stairs, her head just above the landing, level with the girl's feet—waited for this futile exercise to end. It wouldn't take long, she didn't think, and she already knew what must happen next. Goldilocks needed silencing. When Georgina had asked, Margaret had said she'd take care of it. Now was the time.

—

Downstairs, Margaret ran water into a tall glass of ice as if preparing refreshments for a guest and then turned to what was left of the fruitcake and cut a modest piece. She had to be sure the girl would eat it all. Too much and Goldilocks might leave the crucial bite uneaten—the piece where Margaret had tucked the sleeping pills in.

At the second-floor landing she set the glass down on a windowsill and pulled the key out, all her actions steady and deliberate as if she'd done this before. As if prisoners, in that house, were an everyday affair. When she got to the third floor, she stood outside the locked room and listened.

Nothing. Margaret smiled. Just as she'd predicted, the girl had worn herself out.

She put the key in and turned it, the old lock sluggish as it withdrew the latch from the door frame, the heavy door giving a little tremor as it sprang free. And before she could admit to herself what madness this was, Margaret turned the handle and pushed it open just enough to see in. And there she was. Naked and golden across the bed.

As Margaret approached, she saw that the house had done the job for her, just as she'd known it would. Had knocked the girl out with this blazing hothouse of a room. She was splayed on her back across the bed, both arms flung out, and the first thing Margaret noticed was that her breasts were so full and round. Margaret wondered if they were artificial and bent to look, because she'd never seen implants before and her husband, periodically, suggested she should get some. She'd read that they were supposed to be hard and tight, but these breasts looked soft. Inviting. They trembled when Goldilocks breathed out. Margaret could see downy hairs tracking down and across the girl's stomach and around the tiny blip of her navel and she couldn't take her eyes from what those spread legs were offering up, all shaved and glistening.

Goldilocks was older than Margaret had thought she was. Early twenties, probably. But nothing about her body—Margaret looked her over again—had been used up yet. Even those bruises on the inside of her upper arms were such vibrant shades of purple they looked splendid and magnificent, and Margaret, who'd never felt attracted to another woman, wanted to fall on top of this one. Wanted to feel that body pushed against her own, and it thrilled her to think that David might have been with them both in the same day. That Goldilocks, the smell and taste of her, might have been all over him when he'd laid the same blows on her.

Margaret had known her husband had been building to a climax but this—the way she wanted the same dose of medicine she'd directed him to—was new. A surprise. She'd meant for Goldilocks to have taken the brunt of David's escalating mania, and then she would only have to take what was left to bring him back down to a relative sanity. She and this girl were supposed to be the double dose meant for landing him, but they were not meant to land one another. This attraction, as Margaret took in every beautiful inch of this creature, was pure and visceral and as unexpected as the girl herself.

Margaret picked her way carefully down the staircase, shoulder running along the wall because her hands were too shaky to hold the railing. Left foot, right foot to meet it and then left foot again. She'd left the cake, she'd locked the door, and she had no plan for what would happen next. For when David went back upstairs for more. For what that could mean for the two of them.

19

Roz's house, Pippa thought. That's where she needed to go.
She could use the phone and tell someone to come and
pick her up. Keeping the cathedral on her left, she turned back.
The contractions had stopped and her mind was clear for the
first time in months, and the trail made sense to her now. She
recognized features that, even after all the years, had scarcely
changed—a tumble of rocks below a face jagged from a slip, the
cleft where snowmelt gushed in the spring. And Roz's fence
when she came to it hours later was just as she'd remembered it,
even if a little more worn and ramshackle and hidden deeper in
the trees.

The swimming pool was there, deadfall from the storm spinning on its surface—leaves and twigs and branches—the water a
pale green and lapping up over the edge. They were never very

good at keeping it clean, she thought. It was the chemicals. Roz's stepmother was always talking about how bad the chemicals were and threatening to turn it into a natural pond. Biofilter, she called it. Pippa stood on the top step in the shallow end, thinking about a swim. She was so hot and so tired from the long battle to get there, from the trail and the woods and the baby fighting her all the way, the spotty labour, her skinned knees and shredded palms. It had been a long time since she'd swum in this pool. Summers, sleepovers, boys—it was all coming back to her and she wanted to plunge into it and float suspended there, among those memories. She just wanted to go back. Far, far back and away to when just talking was enough. At night she and Roz used to skinny-dip, the cold pinching at their nipples, daring the world to discover them. What a difference now, she thought. No innocence, no modesty—all just equipment meant to service or be serviced. The contractions had stopped but they'd start up again. As a machine, her body was reliable. She took another step down and pushed out, the water cresting in front of her, and floated into the deep end like an inflatable trying not to flip. It felt marvellous, taking the weight off and letting the water carry her for a while. She should've birthed her children in a pool and avoided her legs hauled up to the ceiling, her spine mashed into a padded board and all those people clustering and trying to clean her up, fussing around like fruit flies, feeding off her ripeness.

I should have my baby here.

She gave a push. Nothing yet. Pippa held on to the side and stretched her legs behind her and kicked. She could have her baby here, or she could just slip under herself and let it all go. Hold her breath and never draw another one. She tried, but she was like a cork and there was nothing on the bottom to hold on to. Nothing to stop herself from floating up, no drowning hook. What she'd need was an anchor, pockets full of stones, concrete shoes, an exoskeleton of brick. What she'd need was to have planned it out, but lack of planning, she'd already established, was what her problem was. Her adolescence had just been an uncontrolled slide into adulthood and there was another baby coming now and she didn't want any part of it. Didn't even know whose child it was.

Pippa tried the back door but it was locked and without even thinking she went around the side to the basement door, because it was never locked, and she let herself in. She and Roz had done it so many times after parties or dances, and now she relied on muscle memory to find her way in the semi-darkness to the next room and the stairs. Nothing there had changed.

But the kitchen, upstairs, was different. When had they done that? It took her a moment to find the refrigerator because it wasn't where it used to be against the wall of the basement stairwell. They'd put cabinets there instead. Other things were different too, or had she just misremembered them. How long had it been? She turned to the wall where all the jars of pasta and raisins and nuts and rice should have been, but a big mirror was hanging there instead, and when Pippa caught sight of herself, wet and filthy and huge, she was horrified. She didn't want to see herself, not like that. She was hideous. She grabbed two bananas from the bowl on the island and went to the table at the other end of the room, surrounded by windows, and sat down. This, at least, was the same. A smaller, newer table but at least it was in the same place. Finally, she could feel a settling.

Pippa didn't see him right away. He was stealthy, as children are, moving from the doorway to the chair opposite her before she even knew he was there.

Hi, she said, surprised.

She looked at him. He was young, probably three years old, his T-shirt riddled with dinosaurs.

I'm Philippa, she said. Roz's friend. Who are you?

She tried to remember Roz's extended family. Her cousins. Didn't they live in California? Were any of them still this young?

But he just sat there and was silent. One of her own boys was about his age but she felt no impulse to mother this one. What she wanted was her friend. She wanted to confide in her. Tell her, finally, what had happened. Tell her everything she should have told her such a long time ago.

Where's Roz?

And then he came to life, shooting from his chair and running, screaming, all the way back upstairs. She could hear him, his little feet overhead, the master bedroom, and then the disjointed sounds of an adult and then heavier footsteps on the stairs coming down. He was bringing someone. Pippa winced. Roz's stepmother wouldn't be happy. She'd never been good with surprises.

But it wasn't Roz's stepmother, or Roz, or Roz's father or anyone else Pippa had ever seen before.

Who are you?

The woman clung to her son's hand, for that's who she was—his mother—the two of them imitations of one another, small and petrified.

20

David stirred both mugs of tea and carried them to where his wife was lying immobile in the family room. Georgina was fetching Philippa from Roz's house—which he thought odd, because hadn't both parents died and the house been sold?—and Jax was upstairs on his computer, so it was a chance, for the moment, to be still. To take a deep breath before the next attack, which was the only way to view the current state of affairs with his children camped out in his house like scouts from an invading army. He only ran his clinics on Tuesdays and Thursdays and so, being Sunday, there'd be another entire day of this before he could escape. His wife had the television tuned to the news network, sound down low, and when David set her tea down on the coffee table where she could reach it, she didn't ignore him the way she usually did. Instead, she turned and sat up.

This is different, he thought, trying not to look at the enormous screen at the far end of the room, the sudden flashes of colour, the announcers' faces close up and mesmerizing. Trying to focus only on his wife because he could sense her intensity and he was trying to save his energy for the larger battles that were coming. Better, he knew, to make it at least appear that he was listening.

David, she said quietly. Do you remember that first time?

Her voice was like a whispered incantation because they never spoke about their encounters—those regular episodes of violence that stitched their marriage together. The mug David was holding suddenly didn't feel hot at all. He could have stuck his fingers in and not felt them burning.

There was—, she continued, not waiting for him to respond because she knew she had to keep talking if she was going to let the secret out. I was pregnant.

Pregnant?

I lost it, Margaret said.

She couldn't shy away now. Being honest was her price for getting Pippa back; the vow she'd made to herself—*if Pippa is found, I'll let my secret go.*

It was a boy. There was enough to—

But she couldn't. Not the tiny fetus she'd birthed that night, alone, her husband sleeping, wrapping it in a towel and burying it at the bottom of the hole he'd dug for the magnolia. The hole he'd dug too deep anyway, trying to work through the thrilling horror of what he'd done to her in the middle of the day. How completely he'd given in to his appetite, and how she hadn't fought back.

A boy? He might have had a son, and not just girls he'd named for boys.

Margaret watched him. He was staring at the television, slumped into the couch, everything slack. She had kept that secret to use it as a weapon one day, and now she'd just handed it to him. Like a gift.

I don't—, he began.

Jax burst in holding the phone.

It's Pippa, she said. George's taking her to the hospital.

She had to say it twice before they heard.

Margaret stood at the cliff's edge letting her cigarette burn down and stared out over the city, down to the hospital where Pippa was. It was afternoon and everything was bright.

I'll stay here, she'd said to her husband, making him go. Pushing him gently out the door, as if greeting his newborn grandchild would make up for what she'd robbed him of—a son, which was what she knew he'd always wanted. What he never tired of telling her.

On the other side of the lake where the escarpment boomeranged toward Toronto, she could see a single road cut straight up like a ski run and on it were flashes like beading mercury—cars, lives, destinations. It was easy to feel insignificant with the world spread before you like that. Easy to think that your particular artery of this entire corpus was a redundancy, that it could be severed and nothing would even register the pain. That nothing mattered. That it was blemishes like that—the road carved into the cliffside—that were meaningful and permanent. Original. But Margaret knew better. Knew that what she was doing now—forcing herself into the centre of it, raising her arms like a prophet, like an embrace, like a mother sweeping her children to her breast—that was where the meaning was. Individual families. Home. The very stones around the hearth. It was, after all, why she'd stayed. This was the maelstrom she'd created, and she wouldn't have it any other way—especially now that she'd seeded it with more turbulence than she alone had the power to direct. Her desire to be dominated had always been as strong, or stronger, than her husband's desire to dominate, but now, looking back at the house, she knew there'd been a shift. That girl upstairs, and Margaret's power over her, was something wonderful.

Another baby, she sighed, turning back to look down at the hospital. Philippa's made two more than me. Perhaps now she'll stop.

Even now, Margaret refused to count the boy.

Pippa had jammed her feet into an old pair of her nephew's running shoes, Jax's flip-flops busted from all the rough walking. The sneakers were almost big enough. If her feet weren't so swollen from the pregnancy they'd probably fit perfectly. When had that happened? That her nephew's feet were the same size as hers? It was painful to walk, everything needling her, and the baby so low now she had to shuffle wide-legged like a toy. If she'd been able to turn around she would have seen the debris falling and the trail she was making—leaves and dirt and bits of tree, but all she could manage was straight ahead and even that was difficult. If there'd been a wheelchair, she would have sat on it. A gurney, even better. A hospital. *Thank god.* What had she been doing out there in the woods, and floating in that pool? Why had she thought Roz would be there? Roz lived in Toronto now. She'd visited her half a dozen times.

She let her sister undress her, no fight left. She'd do whatever they said, take whatever she was told to take. Give herself over, because she was so clearly shit at doing anything on her own. She sank back into the plastic mattress and when the nurse lowered the sheet and smeared gel on her mounding stomach, apologizing cheerfully for how cold it was, Pippa just lay back and closed her eyes, glad that someone was in charge of her. Surrendering.

There she is, the nurse said, turning the screen so Pippa could see.

She.

It was all Pippa would remember of that visit to the hospital. After four boys her baby, finally, was a girl. She hadn't even dared to hope. It suddenly didn't matter who the father was, not now. He'd given her a girl and that made up for everything. A fresh start. It was what she'd been looking for and now she had it, this girl, this daughter, a template for a life lived over again. A perfect sheet to map her future on.

By the time David and Jax arrived, Pippa was being discharged because her labour wasn't far enough along and the psych evaluation, the nurse said, had come back "sane enough." The hospital was putting her out, and Pippa was glad for it. All she wanted just then was to collapse, and she would, just as soon as she got home—and not to New Zealand, and Leo and the kids, but up to that house so filled with the past ghosting her, because there were things she had to settle now. How had she forgotten about the lake? That family friend and the culmination—she suspected—of his wanting her for years. She realized now that she'd been running ever since. Covering her tracks with organic grains, a confusion of wholesomeness, laying a bed of moss that would creep and grow, softly obliterating what she'd done—or had done to her. And wasn't it both? She couldn't claim victimhood because hadn't she wanted it too? Encouraged him, enjoyed the illicit adventure at the start? Getting married, having babies, building a family . . . it wasn't until the swinging—the other couples—that she'd remembered having been shared like that before.

She knew she loved them—Leo and the boys—but everything had just happened like the tide rolling in and all of a sudden she'd realized the water had gotten deep. She was tired of treading and she'd forgotten how to swim, and there weren't any sisters down in New Zealand to keep her afloat. Her house was all boys. And boys—she got into her father's car, reached for the seatbelt—were not girls.

This one, she thought, pulling the belt across her tummy, will love me unreservedly. Just the two of us against all those boys and we will win.

Pippa smiled then. The first real smile in weeks.

Her father directed the car out of the parking lot and up the hill for home, saying the right things—how pleased he was to have her back. That a girl—he winked awkwardly when she told him—wasn't the worst you could get. Trying, for her sake, to put a brave face on it and to suppress what was eating him; the crime his wife had confessed to. Never considering, even momentarily, that he was responsible.

Where are the others? Pippa asked.

Said they had something to do, her father replied.

Pippa's thoughts turned to baby showers, sure that her sisters had gone shopping for gifts.

21

The gallery took a little finding because it was in a part of the city Georgina never visited. She'd never thought there was anything worth stopping for in that neighborhood: abandoned storefronts, warehouses, and the streets like canyons that in winter funneled ice and snow and air so cold it sliced your lungs. But this was summer, and the air Georgina stepped out into was so heavy with moisture, the gallery's large windows ran like a waterfall.

She hesitated.

Re-Inventing Rich. A dollar sign with arms and legs, the S climbing a body so thin it was like a dime turned up on edge. Amanda Courtland was the artist. The name didn't sound familiar, but how could she be expected to remember names when her whole working life was a never-ending cascade of them. And all so repetitive and similar. *Alison Howland, Amani Compton, Amy Torston . . .*

Slant rhymes. Phonetic cousins. Georgina stood there, taking the poster in, confused by its use of colour—all shades of yellow. What did that have to do with wealth? Was it meant to represent gold? Searching for some sort of rubric by which to measure things. Feeling stupid and out of place on that deserted sidewalk with her modest professor's car parked at the curb, sandwiched between delivery trucks. She was early, but the gallery's door was unlocked.

Once inside, she began at the extreme left, like a text, and walked slowly alongside the long, high walls of what must have been a warehouse before it was whitewashed. She was reading the paintings. Looking at the Art. And it should have been enough, for her, to see the historical references the artist had woven into the barely figural scenes of luxe and prosperity. Should have been enough to see her lessons taken so to heart— the colourful shadows, the abstract forms and patterns, the depictions of bourgeois leisure fixed there with acrylic spray. Because here it was. Her legacy. Her teaching made manifest. It is, she thought with a start, a lexicon and I can read it like a syllabus. It's Art History 1A03 with an overlay of graffiti.

But it wasn't enough, of course, to recognize that there. Not even close. It didn't even come *close* to validating what she did— all the contact hours, the lectures ad infinitum, the scholarship honed to a razor's edge—it cheapened it. Showed it up for what it was—derivative. How like a jingle, and that the product she sold—creativity—was reduced to an ad. I'm the pitch person, she thought. Not the maker, just the vendor. *That's* the economy on display here, feeling at once drunk and sick at the realization of the part she played. Dreading the artist. What would she say to her? *Re-inventing rich as pastiche* . . . the word sticking in her throat. More jargon to lay the bricks on, cement the wall, these canvases a pretty version of what she'd thrown and buttered, year after year, her entire adult life. Mediocrity. A forti-*fucking*-fication of mediocrity.

Coming here had been a mistake. Just like everything else that day, and the day before.

She went back out to the street and, like a magnetic needle, spun immediately to the escarpment that rose like an arrested tidal wave above downtown, an ever-present threat of extinction. And perfectly on axis with where she stood was the house. Even from this distance it was enormous. Not a house at all, but something grander, like a manor. A palace. And it wasn't hard to imagine that what surrounded her, down there where she stood, were the toiling vassals who sent the constant stream of their tribute up to that ancient citadel. And this art, then, became just another small portion of the estate that wouldn't yield. An acceptable loss that wouldn't even register in the tallies, and could be forgotten because it would never stand the test of time. Because wasn't that house, she felt then, looking up at its windows dazzling in the sun, the polestar? There was no escaping it. Even Toronto wouldn't be far enough away because there would always be that pull from that altitude where even the oxygen was more pure and plentiful. And what—she felt herself slipping now—was the point of something like this? Another failed crop. And wasn't her life, just as it was, good enough? And didn't it produce?

Georgina didn't want to be on that lane skirting the potholes, but where else could she go. Her own house—her husband and son—didn't fit in to any of this. She hadn't even thought about them since this all began, and there had to be a reason for that. The gallery had made her feel worse about her career, but no better about that recurring theme of hers—walking away from it—because there wasn't enough of a difference between the two to justify the effort. She wondered if she was too filled with precedents now, from decades in the academy, to ever see anything as an original ever again. Doomed to copies, how could she ever produce something genuine?

Even this house, she thought, slowing down and easing her car through the gate and along the drive, is derivative. Even my father, standing there and staring me down, is a caricature. And yet . . . *we all came home when trouble sounded*. Answered immediately when that clarion call went out. Was there something valuable at the root of *that* cliché? The trope of "blood is thicker than water"? Or was it just a matter of "keep your enemies close"? She watched her father go back into the coach house as she rolled past, thankful he hadn't chosen to confront her about where she'd been. All she wanted was a cup of coffee and something to eat. A few minutes of peace before Pippa's baby came and sent them all back down to the hospital again. Because she knew it was coming, and soon.

She swung her car in next to her father's, not hopeful about the chance of coffee and food and peace. Of avoiding the questions about where she'd gone and what she'd been doing and why hadn't she come back when Pippa and Jax and their father had— and why hadn't she told anyone? A barrage of recriminations she expected the minute she went inside. The house might be the polestar, but my family, Georgina groused, are careening meteors.

But the house she returned to was not the house she had left.

22

Jax hadn't told anyone where she was going. She'd slipped away when no one was looking because it was none of their business and she didn't want to explain. They were assholes, anyway, especially George, who'd try to stop her from going anywhere or doing anything unless it involved the precious Pip. But Pippa was on her way back up to the house now and they'd had official word from doctors *and* a psychiatrist that she was fine, so—*fuck it*—time to have some fun. She cracked her back, arms still sore from that stupid maniac paddle in the Gulf. Leaving the hospital, she walked north toward downtown, letting the other pedestrians carry her along the crowded sidewalk. She'd changed the plans, a flurry of emails, and now she and Billy were meeting for an afternoon pint because why put it off when they were both there, staying with family, and desperate for a break. His parents, she remembered, were suffocating. When they'd dated in high school his mother had shoehorned her into his all-boy family like a daughter, confiding intimate details of her marriage over cups of tea while Billy and his father were sent to fetch a missing ingredient.

Fuuuuuuuck, Jax exhaled. No surprise he'd moved to Singapore halfway through university.

When we're both married, he'd told her over the phone from his room on Shenton Way, *we'll leave them and be together.*

She walked west now. She felt loosed to the city, like a teenager again. The corner stores, the gourmet cookie shop, the Episcopal church and its portico where she used to shelter when it rained. The old customs house turned into a club, the side street where the hookers worked, the salon where she'd had her hair streaked red the summer after eleventh grade. So many memories like snow falling and sitting on her lashes, turning to ice, freezing her mind. Her muscles, only her muscles, moving her forward now. "The Hammer" was the city's nickname; its citizens imprinted with its beaten streets, with its mistimed traffic lights and dingy storefronts and walk-up windows selling pizza slices, falafels and lottery tickets. Even the people seemed bent as old nails, sorting and re-sorting themselves as they crossed streets and entered and exited stores, rusty and grim. Detritus of the job site, left behind when the city's walls were raised by steelworkers whose descendants still worked the shifts their fathers and grandfathers had. The record store, the upstairs reggae club, the year-round farmers' market with its immigrant foods, the dive Billy took her to once or twice to play pool, young and dangerous . . . and down there somewhere at the city's edge, slate-grey, the lake. Always a boundary, cold and unfriendly, a massive confused unfurling of industry like a canvas painted in sludge, brush strokes sculpted with a trowel. This was her city, and she loved it.

She kept moving, every vector the start of a new memory because she'd learned the Hammer's streets by bus, bike and walking and saw all the shortcuts and alleys, shaded sidewalks for summertime and the shelters she'd cowered in during winter. She saw that long summer afternoon she and Billy ditched school to ride the buses out to Gage Park in the east end to play in its splash pad. Hours of making out, and lying side by side on the grass to let the sun dry them enough to go home.

You're the first girlfriend, he'd told her, *who's fun to hang out with.*

And beyond downtown, if she kept walking to where Lake Ontario shallowed up and took in water from creek-bottomed ravines and boggy fields, was Cootes Paradise. Acres and acres of water and trees that, if you framed your view to cut the city out, hadn't changed for a century. She remembered a winter when she'd skated there, the ice so thick she could glide from one side to the other a mile away. It must have been a sudden winter because the water had frozen completely flat and hardly any snow had lain across it and on the far side, in an inlet between an allée of poplar trees, she'd seen fish swimming lazily beneath the ice. Grasses waving underwater as they passed. She remembered lying flat on her stomach and watching that secret world, wondering how the fish could breathe, marvelling at how fat they were, that they were still alive. And she had taken him. Down the cross-country trails she'd memorized by running through the woods in summertime, showing him the way, holding their blades and sliding down the slick frozen hills, balancing against each other to put their skates on, fumbling because it was cold and because this was still new—being alone together and during the day. Not at a party, not with friends, not drinking or smoking pot or listening to music with no pressure to talk. No communal jokes or banter. They'd held hands before the sky and the beauty of the trees and the entire world frozen there as if that was enough. As if they didn't need the back seat and the kisses and the blowjobs and fingerings and all the rest of it. As if all they needed was this—companionship. Maturity. An equal footing. Somewhere to stride forward from.

I raced him, she remembered, and won. I left him far behind.

But couldn't they start over again? Sex. It'll be worth having waited for. Jax knew she should think about her husband and kids, a montage of them crying, but she couldn't picture them at all. And didn't want to. What she wanted was pure sensation. Music flooding through headphones, vibrations in her feet, a flavour in her mouth. A squall.

Love? Perhaps. Why not.

The Gown and Gavel was just as she remembered it. A tall brick house converted to a pub, the large patio in front with flagstone paving, and the stained glass with its whimsical coat of arms over the front door: a wigged judge grasping the handle of a beer tap. They'd spent so many nights here during high school that everyone knew to show up at the start of an evening, arriving singly or in groups, so obviously a few years underage but no one carded them because pub culture, even in Canada thousands of miles from the mother country, was generous. The proprietors understood the need to drink at any age, and they looked after their regulars.

It was Billy who recognized her first. She'd walked right past him on the street, too busy scanning the patio to notice the man walking out from the parking lot behind the pub.

Jax.

She kept walking, not hearing him.

Jax Attack? he said. His nickname for her.

She turned then, off balance, twisted unattractively, trying not to fall to the side.

Hey, she said. Hey.

She lurched, bumped her forehead against his chin and kicked his foot with her shoe as they hugged and fell back, his hands going to the pockets of his walking shorts, trying to look casual. He was wearing sandals. Not the black Docs she remembered, or the leather jacket, and his hair was cut close instead of gelled. They stood there smiling self-consciously, waiting for some sort of cue they weren't getting, laughing about the collision.

Should we—? Jax backed toward the patio, letting him go first, choose the table, sit down.

So, she said once they were seated. Let's hear some Chinese.

He laughed. What do you want me to say?

I don't know. Whatever. Talk about—. She waved her hand, indicating everything. Was she giggling?

As he spoke, a few sentences in Mandarin, she laughed and made him keep going. More, she cried, tears in her eyes. Don't stop! And he was laughing now too and they were those jack-asses again, teasing the only Asian girl in their grade because it was something easy they could laugh about together, something that was always there, in front of them, a prop. And the girl was too shy to ever fight back.

Too funny, Jax said, wiping her eyes when the waitress came to take their order. That is too funny.

Yeah, he smiled, his demeanour changing. We do a lot of business with Beijing.

But she didn't want to know about that—his life, his job, where he lived. She only wanted to go back, refilling their glasses from the pitcher, deflecting the questions he posed about her job and what she did now. Changing the subject, looking around the patio and talking about how everything and nothing had changed.

The trees, the bar, the—

But you look the same, he said.

It caught her off guard and she couldn't help herself. Are you married? she blurted out.

He looked at her. Really looked at her.

Nope, he said finally, sitting back. And then he spoke in Chinese, and grinned rakishly, and she imagined he'd said *I've only ever loved you.*

What did you say? she squirmed, girlish, sitting forward, breasts shelved on the table, trying to think of a sexy comeback because she wanted to keep things light, and the track they were on was a good one, and they were heading back. She reached out, grabbed his hand, and he gave her fingers a little squeeze and then he reached for her glass, holding it out for her to take instead. That grin again.

She didn't know how it happened. They were on their second pitcher and had ordered a basket of fries, sliding right back into high school and university days. Billy went first, but Jax couldn't wait, so she told the waitress she'd be back and went inside, halfway up the stairs to the landing with the door to the ladies' room. When she came out, Billy was coming down from the men's room on the second floor.

Anyone playing? she asked him, glancing up. Innocent.

Billy stopped and turned and she was already behind him and they went together to look, but it was dark and the door was closed, but not locked, so they pushed in anyway. The sour smell of old beer, the empty floor, the blacked-out windows— one end of the room cordoned off with microphones and speakers where the band would have been if it was a weekend night—the service bar in the back all locked down, its liquor bottles behind bars. And he took her then, in his arms, and they danced. A stumbling silly giggling waltz neither of them knew the steps for and it careened them across to an alcove where the gumball machines and the automatic photo booth were and, without a word, they ripped into each other. It wasn't so much sex as it was savagery. And she wanted it. So badly he had to put a hand across her mouth as he fucked her every way he'd ever dreamt of doing and she thrust her ass at him for more.

Remember what you said? she asked him when they were finished. About divorcing and being together? She whispered it into his chest, forcing it through his shirt with her teeth, afraid to look at him, cum pooling in her underwear.

He wrapped his arms as far around her as he could and squeezed and she knew, from the steadiness of it, from the firmness of his grip, that he was buying time. That he didn't remember anything. That she might even have made it up.

Thank you, he said after a minute. He kissed her forehead, her face between his hands like she was a little girl. Thanks for—

You're welcome, she heard herself saying. As if she'd just been paid.

At least, she thought, I had the courage to do it. As if that made it all right.

23

In that room with the twining wallpaper and the windows out to the treetops and sky, Pippa lay counting the angles in the ceiling, trying to work them out. A jog for the chimney, another for a closet and one, in the corner, that must mask a pipe. Architectural overlays to hide the bones. None of the angles were a perfect ninety degrees, nothing a ruler would favour, and even the windows weren't parallel to the floors or the walls or the crown moulding that edged the room. Everything was crooked. She'd never noticed that before.

She'd thought she could dismiss the lake and the sex and what came of it, that it would just go away, but it had stayed with her so deep down inside it had taken years to work its way out. Like shrapnel. The coarse voice rasping in her ear and the big hands steadying her slender teenage hips. His strength, the twist of his face when he came, the way he'd looked at her afterwards—triumphant—before swimming out away from shore into the moonlit water without another word, leaving her there to figure out what to do next. To get out. To go inside. To change. To sit at the table, she remembered, and join the card game in the kerosene light, laughing with the rest of them, feeling incredible. Rebellious and dangerous and . . . And she'd wanted it. Shameful, how much she'd wanted it. And every time afterwards—hadn't she wanted it then too? Even as he became more and more perverse and demanded things that, at the end, she hadn't been able to give? Things that he'd taken from her anyway?

Pippa had met her husband on the catamaran he was piloting, his uncle's business, running day trips out into the Bay of Islands for paying customers. He came from a farming family, big, powerful men who'd come out from Scotland generations back to clear and settle the land themselves. To get a piece of the colony. The ocean, for those men, was what brought the weather and it was never welcome. They cursed it for every gale and winter storm that hit the farm, blamed it for every irregularity in the stock, every blemish traced back to a frost or wind or flood the bloody ocean had driven in. They'd had one year—they still shouted about it—when that skeeving blasted water sent hail so big it smashed the barn to smithereens and killed fifteen sheep besides. But Leo's uncle had never gone for that view of things and he'd stepped to the coast, apprenticing himself to a boatbuilder until he was old enough to go it alone in the boat he'd built from nothing. *Chastity*, he'd called it. Pippa and Leo still laughed about that name.

They'd anchored offshore of an islet and Leo, with Pippa and the other five tourists, had swum across the shallow lagoon with food and drinks balanced on their heads, struggling to keep their lunch dry, shouting in three languages they were going down, laughing so much they nearly choked. Up from the beach, in the shade, Leo sat next to her. He'd noticed her straightaway and divided her from the herd, nipping at her heels, circling, watching how her body bounced on the waves, imagining her bouncing on top of him. He let her think the catamaran was his. It was a travel fling, not supposed to lead anywhere but bed—he could let her believe whatever she wanted to. And anyway your legs, he told her later on their wedding night, should take all the blame. They're magnificent.

They'd climbed to the highest point, the catamaran below fading to red in the middle of the pacific blue, bobbing in the scalloped bay, and Leo told her stories—cobbled-together tales of Maori and Pakeha, none of them exactly right, but it wasn't important because she was interested and he was just trying to keep her there. He'd tell her anything. Pippa listened, watching the waters come to life with war canoes and mythic fish and tales of cannibalism, pride and victory, conquest and strength, Leo's voice seducing her and they'd had sex, right there, while the others were having lunch. Not even a rock for cover. Just the island beneath them for a bed and the sky for a canopy.

Everything, with him, had felt natural. Marriage felt right. He was youth and exuberance and delight. He was the sun. He was the sparkling of shallows and the glistening of webs that ran past the horizon. Possibility, anew. He was the joy that would never end. The story she most wanted to believe in at the time.

A daughter, Pippa thought, staring at the ceiling, flaking paint, decorative hook. She'll blow it apart and there'll be two of us, polarities. We'll bring balance, and a reckoning.

I'll have my daughter here, in Canada. She'll have a choice. A foothold somewhere else.

And even the sound of breaking glass couldn't tear her from this reverie. Nor could the pounding; nor what happened next.

It was strange that David should do this, take the route up to the third floor to go across and down the other stairs to his bedroom and his bathroom to shower, but nothing about that day had been regular. Once in a while he'd do it to check on things: the ceiling to look for evidence of leaks, each room to make sure the lights were switched off and the doors open to let the air circulate, but this time he wasn't looking at anything in particular. He wasn't attending to his investment, he was just wandering through this house he was king of, to the upper reaches of it, to where it offered him the largest view. When he paused at the top of the stairs and looked out of the window, down to the city and the lake, he imagined himself in the middle of that blue immensity of water swimming like he'd done as a boy. Diving in and swimming down and seeing how far he could go on just one breath, until the light dimmed and he could feel the cold water sitting at the bottom, frightening him to the surface. He supposed you could swim in that lake. The girls swore it was too polluted and made you itch, but if you took a boat out to the very middle of it, wouldn't that be fine? Not the rivers of his youth, but fine. A son. A son would have done that very thing. *Everything I've done and more.* This was what he'd been cheated of—another chance. The girls had always favoured their mother over him, but a boy, a boy would have naturally favoured him. Not this coven—he felt his knuckles whiten on the windowsill—this bloody bitching coven I've spent my adult life in. I could have been *out there*—he rapped the glass until it broke, not even considering the pool and its vinyl liner down below, punching at the pieces still holding to the glazing until his fingers were lashed with blood, until the window frame was mostly clear, until he could feel the wind the great lake kicked up to the mountain's top.

A boy. My kingdom for a boy.

It wasn't until he turned away for something to stanch the bleeding, that he saw the little heap of clothing his wife had dropped outside the door. Those cheap lace panties a perfect match for the bra he'd taken. He twisted them around his wounds, holding them to his nose, sliding his tongue across them and tasting sex. More bitterness. More of what he deserved just beyond his reach. *Always*, he thought, *kept unfairly beyond my reach*. And he fell against the door to steady himself and knew, from the way it resisted him, that it was locked

Locked?

He tapped softly with his fingertips. Drumming the line of them like a meditation. He tried the doorknob. And then he thundered at the wood with both fists. Margaret, in less than a minute, was at his side. Swift when she needed to be. And when she drew the key from her pocket and he looked at her, stupefied, she realized he didn't know anything about Goldilocks being there. That the girl was a surprise, a novelty, for *both* of them. That Goldilocks was *her* doing, not his. And that changed everything.

Margaret saw that Goldilocks had eaten the cake. It explained her prone across the bed, face down and breathing shallowly, her shoulders scarcely moving. As she and David crept forward together, Margaret closing the door behind them, they both saw the crisp red apple tattoo on the girl's bottom, and in their heightened state, they looked at each other and snickered.

It's okay, Margaret whispered, putting a hand against her husband's leg. I've made sure it'll be okay.

And David didn't need to ask what she meant by that; he knew. And he turned to his wife then, beaming, and wanted to kiss her. She'd known all along how much he'd wanted this, and she was *giving* it to him. Had arranged everything. He pulled his wife to his chest so she could feel his benevolence, his gratitude. He wanted to say something, a perfect bon mot, a benediction, but she pushed back before he could utter them and he watched, spellbound, as she knelt on the bed beside the girl and ran a hand over her calf and the back of one thigh and the tattoo, small of her back and up to her shoulder and then, in a single unexpected movement, went under and flipped the girl onto her back so that she lay there for the taking—exposed and quivering. His wife cut her eyes at him then, and he knew that look. It was a challenge. An invitation to play. *An apology for having lost my son.*

He dropped the panties he'd been clutching and lowered himself, gingerly, to his knees and took both the girl's feet in his hands and, not taking his eyes from his wife, pried them gently apart, sliding his hands up and crawling forward until he was close enough to bury his face in that delicious smell. Margaret, trembling, moved up the bed and rolled the girl's head into her lap, legs either side, and watched as the girl—stirring now—pulled him even deeper inside herself, moaning with the pleasure of it.

The possibilities had just exploded, and her husband, buried in the girl's pussy, didn't even know it yet.

24

After the last dinner party, Georgina told her husband that she was through with it. That she wouldn't sit on another beige microfibre couch in a room pocked with African threshers and hatchets and other everyday objects of the very poor and powerless raised to the level of collectibles, artfully displayed across the colour-neutral walls. She wouldn't sit, with a belly full of locally sourced fusion cooking, and decry the lack of civility in politics, the misplaced funding, the declining quality of the students they were labouring to teach . . . It was the same tired bullshit every time, the same hollow arguments, the same outrage they doused each other with to warm their hearts. And then, by dessert, they'd all be flipping their scholarship out like bibs on a baby, staking their claims to righteousness, opening their mouths to let their ideas dribble out. Georgina knew she was guilty too. She'd written two books—each one a rehash of other work (*Matisse in Paris*, *Matisse post-Paris*)—and she had a store of quotes she pulled out to refill her glass and continue the toast to their communal excellence, their intellectual superiority, their relevance even though she knew it was just a system they'd invented to avoid doing anything original themselves. They were carrion. Great big flapping oily carrion.

She'd said all of this and her husband, Pieter, had just looked at her, nothing registering. Those dinner parties, she knew, were his finest moments and he'd never give them up. Gorging on the sinews and tendons of someone else's creativity were what his jaws did best. Snap! Snap! He mashed through cartilage. Snap! Snap! He ate through bone. Ate it, shat it, and came reeling back for more. His field, political science, was a charnel house—his job to take apart and reassemble carcasses, and push them on the world as something new. Something vibrant and alive.

Georgina sighed. She stood in the driveway between her car and the big house feeling she was teetering on the verge of something, but without understanding what it was. For someone whose life had been as finely engineered as an aqueduct, this was unsettling. It made the house—with its edifice of tradition and respectability—seem even more solid and comforting, and so when she moved to the kitchen door it was for consolation and reassurance that, like a child, everything would be all right.

This is Goldi, her mother said lightly when Georgina stepped inside, gesturing at the figure walking to the table with a plate of food. The girl from upstairs, Georgina realized. *And wearing my clothes*—a sleeveless silk top and linen shorts, both of which were absurdly small on her.

The girl kept walking, no acknowledgment, and sat down with her back to the room, facing the bay window and the view out, and if it weren't for her elbows working up and down you wouldn't know that she was busy eating. You'd just think she was being rude.

Oh, Georgina said, trying to mask her shock.

She's a stray, Margaret said, dropping her voice, speaking through smoke. From the garden tour. Your father let her in, but I've let her stay.

With that lie, giving Goldi's presence among them a double authority.

I'm washing her clothes, Margaret said, noting where her daughter's gaze had lingered. I had to give her *some*thing in the meantime.

And there it was. That tiny jarring note of anger at being challenged that Georgina knew her mother could ignite, with no warning, into a racing inferno.

Of course, no problem, Georgina said. Laying out firebreaks. Wanting only to slide into that house and get what she needed, too played out already for anything more. There could be twenty strays upstairs and she wouldn't care. Would make a point not to notice, because all she wanted was to be left alone.

Tea? her mother asked loudly, even though she knew Georgina would never say yes. Would always reach for the coffee, which was what she was doing. Cake?

Georgina accepted the large slice of fruitcake and scrabbled around in the drawer to find a fork, settling for a trident-shaped utensil because all the other forks had already been used. In fact the whole kitchen, she noticed now, was a shambles. Dirty plates everywhere and, on the island, what must have been the entire contents of the refrigerator spread across it. Like a Doré illustration for *Gargantua and Pantagruel*, she thought, looking at the jars and bottles and blocks of cheese. There was the platter of roasted chicken and potatoes from two nights ago, a dripping boat of warmed-up gravy and, as if to authenticate the comparison, Goldi came back just then to stack more food onto her emptied plate. Using her hands, single-minded, not even looking at Georgina or her mother, still chewing an enormous mouthful of beet and goat cheese salad that Georgina could see swirling crimson across her tongue. There was a smear of drying gravy across her cheek, glossy with oil.

Georgina glanced at her mother, meaning to share her disbelief at this guest's atrocious manners, but her mother had shrunk back, and the intensity with which she was watching this girl, ready to spring away at the slightest indication of—an attack?—was startling. And Georgina thought that the note she'd detected in her mother's voice must have been fear, not anger. And it was there now, unmistakable.

Excuse me, Georgina said indignantly, putting a hand on the dish the girl was lifting. Instinctively jumping to her mother's defence.

But Margaret's reaction was even quicker. Taking the dish, she tipped its contents onto Goldi's plate while pushing Georgina's hand back and chattering about what else was on offer, as the girl kept grabbing food and piling it up, reaching for more gravy, pouring it over everything. Because Margaret's fear was in fact the fear of Goldi leaving if she didn't get enough of what she wanted.

Georgina sighed.

I'm going for a shower, she said. This stray, not a problem she needed to deal with. She'd had enough of other people's problems and this one was clearly related to her parents and for once, Georgina thought, they can bloody well sort it out for themselves.

Georgina eased the bedroom window's sash up, the sill mid-thigh, and leaned her head and shoulders out into the wind coming up off the city, into the traffic noise and the sirens and the swirling height, and wondered what the point of it was. Of any of it. When would she feel that she had everything in hand? By squinting to varying degrees, she turned the cityscape from impressionism to cubism to abstract expressionism, but still it didn't help, to see that the world could hold all of that at once. That all those people down there were moving over and through a giant living canvas. That living itself might be an art form they were all participants in. She saw Jax next to the pool like a Hockney, and thought that there was the sort of composition she needed for herself. Something flat, where everything had its place. A sort of paint-by-numbers, she smiled weakly, beginning to regain some sense of herself, looking out at the larger world and seeing an endless succession of images reflected back at her. Everything contained. It is, she reminded herself, bolstering her claim to how she lived, all just a reproduction anyway. It can all be learned.

Later, she would stand at the opposite window, dripping and woozy from her shower, and watch them down there: her mother and her father, walking away from the house. Both outside in the failing day moving through different parts of the garden, unaware of each other, like a film. Something period. Something Masterpiece. Tiny splinters of noise would reach her through the open window—the crackle of her mother's feet on the driveway, the click of a tool over her father's way, the sound of a leaf blower out in the neighbourhood somewhere, its whine consistent and pervasive and so commonplace she had to really focus to make it stand out.

From the ground, the garden always looked spontaneous and impossibly vast, but up here you felt you could almost see its limits and make out the different elements that had been so meticulously arranged: a natural copse, a perennial border, formal hedges, a perfect grass circle ringed with herbs. A rose garden delineated with trellis work, and way back, beneath the oaks, the woodland garden with its carefully selected hostas, ferns, rhododendrons and azaleas, each one laid out and planted to complement the others. An ensemble, Georgina thought. A perfect distillation of a library's entire wing. There were volumes and volumes of scholarship concentrated in that landscape's design . . . Jekyll, Brown, Lloyd, Sackville-West—a festschrift of order over chaos. Something willed. There were clematis on the tennis court fence, their blooms like pressed flowers, and paths lined with enormous mounds of lavender that left their scent on your ankle when you brushed against them. When they'd moved there, as children, the land had been grass and trees and they'd played soccer where the flowers were now. Huge sprawling soccer games with tree trunks as the opponents and goalposts and corner flags, until bit by bit the trees had been felled and the soil tilled. Everything stripped away and then embellished, a riot of greenery and butterflies and bees. Even there, at the open window, if she closed her eyes, Georgina could hear the insect multitudes at work.

It was the house, she realized then. The house that had

brought them all back. For it wasn't they who'd inhabited the house; it was the house and its grounds that had colonized them. And wasn't that stray girl, even that girl, some kind of evidence of that? Because hadn't the house always taken people in? Every weekend there'd been teenagers sleeping on the couches and spare beds throughout the house—friends and acquaintances who'd just drifted in by themselves, coming back after parties or last call, because everyone knew the doors at the Blackford place were never locked and that there was plenty of space, and that the house wouldn't turn them away. That they could take refuge overnight and in the morning disappear out into the garden and back into the world and that even though the sisters might hear of it later, the parents would never know. A palatial flophouse with no registry. A shelter for those in need.

Margaret left through the front door. She stepped onto the grass track that wound through what was left of the garden after the tour and began popping the dying blooms off plants. She didn't push into the beds to get at the back, but just worked at what she could reach easily, leaving the snapped heads along the edge as if she meant to go back and collect them and take them to the compost. Pick up her mess. As if this, being out in the garden, wasn't an anomaly but was instead part of her normal rotation of chores. For so long she'd been confined to the house, looking out at her creation being chiselled free of where she'd placed it. Being ground down and simplified, her husband's influence through it like a plague of tiny biting things that nibbled-nibbled-nibbled until the ambition of it, the thrilling complexity, the harmony, was reduced to what she recognized as a jingle of pretty colours and department-store smells. *A man's view. An amateur.*

She remembered, pausing at the lamb's ear hostas, the family of rabbits who used to live in there, but she hadn't seen them for years and sometimes, when she thought about them, she wondered if it was because of the chemical they sprayed to keep the weeds down. The government had banned it but David had stockpiled quantities, and Margaret wondered if they should stop, let those weeds crowd back in and see if the rabbits came back as well. As if a colony of rabbits would balance everything, stop the tilt she felt her world resting on. She had read about bees disappearing and frogs mutating and she wondered how much of that was her fault too, feeling she should go to the coach house now and dump it, all of it. Just get it over with. Send it sailing over the cliff and off the property. She could remember a springtime, years ago, when a duck had brought her new ducklings to the pool to teach them how to swim. For three days the mother had trotted them like a nursery rhyme out of the hostas and daffodils and into the chlorine to paddle around in a wavering stream of yellow fuzz and innocence while Margaret stayed inside, watching them through the glass. Had they died too?

Margaret pulled a cosmos. She supposed it was her fault, all of it. Pippa's breakdown was because of everything she'd done and hadn't done. But Pippa had asked to come home, to feel safe, to get better—surely that must count for something? Haven't I created something wonderful, she thought uncertainly. Something permanent? Another baby was coming and it would come here, for her to hold, its little cries and gripping hands and that small pleasurable weight against her chest . . .

The scarlet petals had fallen and Margaret with them, bent into the soil, her tears like rain onto that small patch of her relentless gardening where every root that took hold was that baby she'd lost. *I should have had a fourth and fifth as well. I should never have stopped.* Because Philippa, as if to punish her, had had baby after baby after baby and mothered all of them. And all of them boys. She'd stayed with them, fed them, loved them, shaped little worlds for them the way Margaret never did. *I just dropped them to the earth and let them crawl.* The tremendous guilt sliding like a glacier and scraping her raw. And she knew it would recede to bide its time before slipping over her, again and again, until she died. Is that what she deserved—all of that? And why—she felt the turning now, the precipice, the rising seas—was the blame all hers? *If David* . . . And just like that, she switched. Stacking reasons and excuses, pushing the glacier back, finding her husband wanting, culpable, guilty but somehow free of it. Contentedly, outrageously free. And after all she'd done for him—all she continued to do.

But now, she thought, *he knows.*

Perhaps this time the push back could be shouldered between the two of them; they could form a sort of dam. Atonement, she thought, grinding the petals into the dirt with her thumbs, is a red herring. It implied salvation from some other source and Margaret, if she knew nothing else, knew that what we are is what we made.

She looked back at the house. She'd made a life out of managing things, out of providing her husband with what he needed to stay functional. She'd tethered herself to his rages to keep them from soaring beyond what was acceptable because what was a family, after all, if not a population in miniature—and every country needed gerrymandering. Someone to pull the puppet strings. And Margaret knew that she needed those flare-ups too. She needed the extremes to jolt her awake because she'd always believed she was born for greatness and just needed waking up to it. Without the occasional violence, life was too much the same.

Margaret's gaze drifted to the attic window and then dropped two floors down to where she'd left the girl in the kitchen, eating all their food. The girl was a professional, that much was obvious, and Margaret had decided to use her services to make everything good again. It would be a delicate business, but Margaret could manage it. She always did.

David glimpsed his wife out in the garden and bent lower over the sprinkler head he was trying, halfheartedly, to fix. Really he was just getting away from the house and everyone in it. He pulled the sprinkler up from its sleeve and turned it back and forth, attempting to dislodge anything that might be blocking the holes. They never worked properly and this one, judging by the wilted peony bushes, hadn't been working at all. He looked at his hand, sure a few of the cuts from that broken window would scar. His skin not what it used to be. Everything so much thinner now.

But what is she doing out here?

David gave up on the sprinkler. He didn't know what was wrong with it; didn't even know the first thing about the elaborate irrigation system he'd paid to have installed and set up to operate independently. He'd have to get someone in to take a look. And because he was afraid to straighten and show himself to his wife, he crouched down on his toes but then lost his balance and tipped over backward onto the lawn. He didn't even try to get up. What was the point. He was hidden, and it was comfortable in the grass on his back like that, his feet over the edge of the bed, his muscles stretched, the fresh green canopy of the oak high overhead with its cables screwed to the limbs to hold them up. Every year the tree company came and he paid them a small fortune to check those cables and make sure they were still preventing the inevitable and catastrophic collapse. David hoped it happened after he was gone because he was used to that old tree, the way it anchored the garden and shaded the beds, and was laced with drifts of snow all winter long like a painting.

He closed his eyes, sure that if he tried hard enough he'd be able to feel his wife as she moved around—their mutual existence defined by those boundaries. By the innate sense they'd both developed, over many years, of where the other one was so they could avoid any overlap. There'd been something he'd done as a kid, something from a cowboy story, he tried to remember—put your ear to the ground to hear the horses before the Indians attacked? His scalp was already tingling. He tried, but the grass muffled everything. If she finds me like this, he thought, she'll think I've had a stroke. The possibility appealed to him and he lay there, motionless, hoping now that she would come. This habit of taking things out on her. But . . . she'd given him a gift. He'd tried to see it as something else—a trap or a bribe, some payback of her own—but lying there, with his whole body pressed solidly into the earth, he knew it was in fact a bounty. A tithe, perhaps, but ultimately something good and grand. Something wonderful that she had gifted him.

His mind began edging back toward that fugue state he flirted with, his tongue running across his lips, desperate to taste it again, the growing ecstasy.

Eat now, he thought crudely, picturing that girl in the kitchen. So ripe for it she was bursting through her clothes.

A gift, he grinned. A prize. A reward he knew he'd earned.

25

Goldilocks was finished eating. For now. She knew the old fucks were outside and that the others were somewhere upstairs, so it was a good time to have a look around the ground floor. She'd run through it so quickly the other day, trying to get away from the man who'd paid her to go on the bus with him, that she hadn't registered much more than the fact that the house was gigantic and stuffed to the cheeks with good shit.

She went from room to room, trailing her fingers across whatever she fancied, thinking giddily that she'd definitely landed on her feet here. *Moneyedfuckingshitisright.* And nobody—she lifted a gilt clock—would miss even a quarter of it. Not the gold paperweight, or the delicate ebony burro, its panniers filled with diamonds, or the jade coasters, or the round frame carved out of amber . . . She lifted them all, cradling them in the crook of one arm and wishing she had a bag. Not believing her luck. Thinking that the fucked-up job she'd taken with that perv who'd said he'd pay her extra for kinky was turning out okay after all, and that even though this new arrangement might not be an actual and official *job*, she'd been in the game long enough to know how to turn it to her advantage. She picked at a small coloured sticker on the base of a gold ballerina, noticing stickers on some of the other objects she held, and laughed out loud at the idea that this was a flea market, everything priced for sale. Tucking the statue under her arm, grinning. She wasn't fooled. She'd bargained for enough trifles to know that these were the real deal. And they were free.

This place didn't just have *curtains*, she noticed—it had entire fucking swags of velvet hanging from its rods and pooling on the floor. It was like a museum. Even the walls were covered with stuff and the wallpaper—Goldi ran a hand over it—was fuzzy. The patterns were in felt that stood out and must have been stuck there by hand. By perfect, tiny hands. The rugs under her feet were soft and thick like marshmallow and there were so many cushions arranged on all the furniture that if she piled them up they'd reach to the second floor, at least. And not shiny satin cushions like she had on her one chair in the two rooms she rented, but cushions that were like cream filled donuts, bursting with a softness she couldn't keep her hands off.

At the top of the first flight of stairs, she looked in at the open door—too greedy to pass it by—and saw it was the old woman's dressing room. A closet that was in fact a *whole room*. There were rows and rows of shoes beneath a hanging extravagance of fabrics, and Goldilocks stepped in and dropped the trinkets in the middle of the carpeted floor to start in on this even bigger treasure trove, in this room the size of a swimming pool.

Evenfuckingreeksoftoomuchmoneyliketheinsideofavault.

She squeezed out of Georgina's borrowed clothes and began trying on Margaret's. Silk charmeuse, cashmere, suede, silver and gold lamé—anything sumptuous, she put on and took off, closing her eyes to the gorgeous feel of the garments gliding over her skin. She got on her knees and pulled out the most outrageous shoes, from every decade—platforms, stilettos, ankle straps, peep-toes, d'Orsays and kitten heels—sliding her feet, finally, into the knee-high midnight blue velvet boots she pulled out from the back. Triumphant. As if she'd found the precise thing she'd been searching for. Four-inch heels and a zipper that disappeared with such intricate craftsmanship Goldilocks knew these boots had been expensive. *Very* expensive. *Fuckingspitebuyforsure.* That was something she knew about. She fingered the jewellery tangled on the dresser in the matching silver boxes, pulled out necklaces and rings and bracelets—all of it as heavy and cold as she always knew rare metals would be—and she draped herself in gold. When David found her there, wearing the boots and jewellery and nothing else, and reaching for the mink stole she'd spied on a high shelf, her bottom out—he pushed her into the bedroom.

Naughty naughty naughty, he hissed eagerly. Jerking the necklaces up across her face like chains to hold her down.

When he was finished, Goldi left him there collapsed into the mattress, surprised by the old man's stamina. But she'd had enough men like him to know they always went at it harder than the young ones did—at least initially. It never lasted. All she had to do was wait it out, and it wouldn't be long before he preferred simple cuddling or harmless schoolyard fantasies, or even nothing at all but just to have her around as something young and vibrant to get a charge off. *Wholejobfuckedupfromthestart.* A bodice-ripper, the client had told her, going on about romance novels and milkmaids and something called pastril? pestril? when he'd put her on that bus. But he'd said nothing about trying to drown her in the swimming pool—which he'd called a pond. Or dragging her into the bushes as if it was an actual rape and not a pre-arranged, prepaid transaction. He'd paid for kinky but what he'd tried for was something more extreme and he hadn't paid nearly enough for that. Ditching him and running inside to hide—she looked around—was working out better than she'd hoped. And it was almost as if she'd been expected. They'd even *fed* her, for fuck's sake. This house had been waiting for someone like her to come along.

She continued her tour, room by room, identifying items she'd return for—certain now, after the old man had come for her again, that she could stay as long as she liked. Even the wife had welcomed her after making sure she wouldn't run—and why would she? This place was a jackpot. She could stay for years and never go through it all.

Goldi passed in and out of other bedrooms, one of them occupied with someone showering in its adjoining bathroom, and Goldi knew it was the woman from downstairs whose clothes she'd been given because she recognized the smell. Goldi rifled through the woman's belongings but there was hardly anything there, and she wondered if perhaps she wasn't the only runaway. Taking note, and ready to fight for the lottery jackpot of this gig if she had to. Goldi went down a hallway next, and through some connecting rooms to another staircase and a bathroom and, around a slight turn, found herself at the room directly below the one she'd been locked up in. This room, she saw right away, was of a different kind. Nothing solid about it. It was the sort of transient jumble that Goldilocks spent her life in, and so she had no interest in it. Nothing there for her. Standing in the middle of it, the boots and jewellery still on, the old man's cum seeping from her, she took a swatch of fabric off the desk and ran it between her legs before throwing the cloth down, his sour smell on her fingertips now. She squatted, pushing, trying to expel the rest of him and thinking that if she was going to stay she'd need some supplies. The wife would have to get those for her. She'll want me clean. The wives, she knew, always wanted you to be clean.

Goldi stood and spun on one foot, kicking her other leg above her head and laughing when it hit the hanging light fixture, making it swing. She could see the wife now, through the window, standing in the grass and staring up at the house. Goldi turned and waggled her backside and then turned again and shook her tits, finally pressing them against the glass, but the old bat still didn't see and Goldi knew it would be a cinch to rob these people blind. They didn't see *anything*. *Fuckingcluelessiswhat*.

She peeked in the room next door and was over the threshold before she noticed the body lying in the bed, facing away. *Another* woman. It was a whole house of fucking women. She backed out just as the body shifted.

George? Georgie, is that you?

Goldi froze. Waiting. Being found there, naked, wouldn't help her plan of screwing these people over, but the voice was weak and sleepy and Goldi was able to back out before she was seen. Able to creep back down the hall to the stairs, and climb back up to her room. She'd seen so many nice things, but now she had to figure out how many of them she could fit because if she was staying, and she was, her room needed some prettying up.

Pippa's eyes were open. She'd been daydreaming, remembering candlelight in that room. An old-fashioned silver candlestick she'd found in a cabinet and jammed a taper into, lighting it at bedtime to read. No one had ever cautioned her about setting the house alight. She didn't think anyone had even noticed. Their mother's cigarettes already filled the house with so much smoke that no one would have marked the smell of wax, or the sulphur of matches being struck. They were, all of them, so used to the smouldering. Pippa thought about how she didn't read at all anymore. Didn't even pretend. She read children's stories but she hated them, and when she could get away with it, when her kids were only listening to the sounds she made and not the sense, she'd turn several pages at once just to skip to the end and get it over with. Talking animals. Fucking mice and bunnies. Always a lesson or a moral or an example of heroism and perfection. Couldn't anyone just look around, Pippa thought, and see how wrong that was? How books and life were two totally different things?

She wanted to tell someone. Tell them everything. Before this baby came, she had to tell someone what had been done to her at the lake because this baby was a girl and the house must be readied to receive and protect her. This girl, like all girls, would be a target too.

Pip?

Georgina, Pippa sighed. Of course.

Were you calling me?

And just like that, after twenty-two years, Pippa freed the torrent of images from the basin she'd sealed them up in, and left her sister gagging for air. For something—a root jutting from an embankment, a hanging branch, a floating log—for some sort of lifeline by which to anchor herself in the time before this flood that was overwhelming her. And not just because of the obvious evil of it—an adult taking advantage of a child—but because Pippa, as the youngest, fell under Georgina's protection too. And Georgina had failed.

26

Jax lay poolside even though the afternoon sun was waning and the air cooling, but everything ached and she just needed some time to rest and recuperate. It wasn't just Billy and the long walk back up to the house dragging the shame of what they'd done, but it was also the kayaking trip and the night's storm and the poor sleeps, and Pippa and the rest of them . . . and so instead of being inside and helping her mother with Pippa, or out in the garden with her father cleaning up the mess, she was lying there making herself drift through happier memories of that house, trying to put herself back together.

She was remembering a huge party, the band setting up right where she was lying now, poolside at the deep end near the diving board. It had started the way parties always start, dates on a calendar when parents will be out of town and friends smirking at you across the classroom or jostling you in the halls, or talking about it at lunch in the coded language of teenagers under the nose of their teachers. A communal push. This party at the Blackford place would be epic. The massive drunken blowout they were always searching for, every weekend and all summer long.

Saturday afternoon, the band plugged their amps and speakers into long extension cords they ran out the library window to the pool deck. The beer started arriving late afternoon, cases of it, bought by kids with fake IDs and stockpiled there in advance, loading both fridges, a few bringing coolers filled with ice. The more paranoid hid their stashes in the garden, where even they would have trouble finding them later, in the dark, when they arrived in their howling carloads. The phone rang constantly: changes of plans, updates, someone's cousin had heard about it from a kid in his math class and now all of the valley, and even Burlington across the lake, knew about the party that one of the big houses on the mountain was having. *Everyone* was coming.

Cancel it, Georgina said when she realized. But there was no stopping it now; it was a juggernaut rolling in. And Jax had told Roz who'd told Billy's friend that Jax liked Billy, and she'd heard back that Billy liked her too. The party, now, was critical.

You're in charge, Georgina, their parents had said when they left for Montreal. We're trusting you. You're old enough.

By eleven p.m., when the police came to unplug the band, cars were parked twenty deep. It was so crowded by then that the officers could have mingled and no one would've noticed them. The band moved into the family room, started playing Steppenwolf—"Magic Carpet Ride"—and Billy raided the freezer, pulling out whole fish and shrimp and pitching them into the swimming pool, laughing maniacally, jumping in after them and doing dolphin kicks, Jax laughing so hard she fell in too. He'd touched her then, fumbling to reach the side, both his hands under her shirt, trying to hold on to her breasts, grinding his hips against her. Hard.

When the band ran out of material, the stereo went on full volume, and as the night wore on and more people arrived and others passed out, and the cans and bottles and cigarette butts and mess piled up, as trysts were formed and broken—as night became early morning—the feeding began. Frying pans were pulled out and eggs cooked and toast made and the refrigerator emptied. Some crept away to sleep and others, a few, the real drunkards, the heroes, the hardcore and enviable and badass few with their cool jeans and T-shirts, kept going and by sunrise, even then, they had beers in hand to toast the coming day. Invincible. The city at their feet. Badge of honour they'd carry for a lifetime. Jax had missed it by an hour, falling asleep in a floating lounger in the pool, Billy pushed in beside her, the two of them all tangled up and a couple now. They didn't need the sunrise anymore.

Jax had to see him again—just to be sure. She dropped her arms over the side of the lounge chair and ran her palms over the concrete deck, just barely feathering it, the sensation focusing her. She swept her hands out in widening arcs, brushing the fingertips of her right hand against the border of zinnias, and if she'd had her eyes open, and been watching, she'd have seen glass shards bouncing and catching the light on the plants she was riffling, because this technicolour profusion of flowers was directly below the window her father had destroyed.

They arranged to meet again, that night for dinner. He hadn't balked. He'd seemed eager, even, and now Jax wondered if she'd misread what had gone down between them as being a transaction when in fact it had been something more meaningful. He'd even suggested a restaurant that hadn't existed when they'd both lived at home—as if he was ready, at last, for a relationship that was grounded in the present.

When we're both married, we'll leave them and be together.

I'm going out, Jax told Georgina, who was already at work on a pasta dish for dinner.

Meet me, Jax had told him, at the bottom of the stairs. The Lodge. She knew he'd remember it because it was the place they'd all gone as teenagers to make out. On Friday and Saturday nights, the small walled parking lot tucked back in the escarpment's trees was so filled with cars it was difficult to get out if you hadn't backed your car into its space. When the rookies flicked their headlights on to start their fifty-point turns, the angry car horns from all the exposed couples bounced off the escarpment and could be heard for miles.

He'd laughed. You know I'm borrowing my mum's car. And Jax immediately pictured the green Volvo station wagon with all its space in the back, and the wool blankets kept there even in summer when the risk of breaking down in sub-zero temperatures had passed.

We might not make it to dinner, she'd countered, laughing too.

—

Not this light, she thought as she opened the car door and the overhead bulb came on. The half-light of early evening under the trees is better for us. And it wasn't the Volvo. Instead, it was a small compact he said his mother never drove because of her bad knees and hips.

Too low to the ground. I've been telling her to sell it, but she won't.

It's her independence, Jax said, tucking her legs up so she could face him as he nosed the car out through the opening in the wall and onto the road.

What is?

He was softer than she remembered. His jawline not as hard as it had been, and under his chin, in profile, the skin sagged and bunched. And his stomach, now that he was sitting, was rounder.

The car, she said. So she doesn't have to rely on anyone for rides.

Like you, eh?

Yeah, she smiled. But I like riding you.

The instant she'd said it, Jax knew it was off and wanted it back. It wasn't suited to the mood or the place or the hour, and was freighted with a crudeness she hadn't intended. She'd meant it as a shared murmur. Something intimate between them, like the old days. Banter.

Billy focused on the traffic, remarking on the restaurant's location and how he was sure there was probably a better way of getting there, but—

Did you say it was Thai? Jax asked, trying to gloss over her mistake. Because I love Thai food.

Well, yes. Although really—his tone shifting into a register she didn't recognize—it's not strictly Thai food. It's more accurately Thai-infused Chinese-American with a few Vietnamese noodle bowls and a Malaysian curry or two thrown in.

Are you gay? she laughed. It was the joke they'd always had about men who obsessed over food.

He reached a hand across and down her shirt and tweaked her nipple. Grinning.

You can't accuse me of that, he said, putting both hands back on the wheel.

And there was the evening: a graph plotted with awkward moments buoyed along on an undercurrent of sexual tension that was the only part of their history that was still as strong, or stronger, than it had always been. They discussed the menu and the view across the lake; they skirted around their real lives and their jobs and their children—for Billy mentioned a son back in China and the woman he'd declined to marry; and by the time the meal was finished and the leftovers boxed up and forgotten on the table, the two of them were marvelling at the new lakefront promenade as they walked, hands on each other, drunk with their predicament. Where to go? They chatted, but neither was listening, each of them searching for a stand of trees or an open shed or even a truck bed. What they found, right at the end of a pier, was a cabin cruiser with enough space at the stern to lie down and be shielded by the two outboard motors and the storage boxes running either side of its deck.

Billy leapt from the dock.

Permission to come aboard, Captain, Jax giggled.

Only—and she could hear the grin in his voice—if you promise you'll blow my whistle.

They were teenagers again.

She bent low, trying to lift the lid of a storage box, and Billy came up behind her.

I'm looking for life jackets, Jax whispered, but it's locked.

We're not going to sink, Billy murmured, grabbing her hips and pulling himself up against her.

Jax turned slowly to face him.

Something soft to lie down on, she whispered.

And I thought you liked it hard, he said, thrusting into her.

Easy, tiger, Jax laughed, backing up as she lifted her shirt over her head and dropped it to the deck. It felt good to tease him. To make him wait. She could see how starved he was.

You want me? she said, coy, backing up against the cabin door as he followed her and snaked his hands around to her back and her bra, their actions so flawless and rehearsed and ages-old, but they were savouring them now. Undressing slowly until they were both, for the first time together, naked.

Jax, he mumbled as he kissed her, eyes closed, their hands delicate on each other's bodies.

This time, the sex was luxurious. And when it was finished and they were next to each other on the deck, their clothes under their heads for pillows, he said, I do remember, Jaxie. Saying that.

Jax rolled into him. It was her turn to stall now. To make him wait, to leave him hoping for something she had no intention of giving because this—infidelity—was a much bigger prize. She didn't have to settle for just Billy, or her husband, or any other man. She could have them all.

27

Pippa hadn't given Georgina all the details, but she'd given her enough that when Georgina went downstairs and through the filthy kitchen to the porch and found their mother sitting there, serene and smoking, she wanted to shift the blame and guilt to her. If an older sister could be responsible, then a mother was undoubtedly *more* responsible.

Did you know about Philippa and Dr. Sanders?

Margaret lowered her cigarette, pushed her hair back from her face.

Malachy? Malachy Sanders?

They had sex. Starting when Pip was a kid.

Georgina watched her closely for any tremor of surprise. Or recognition.

No, they didn't.

Georgina took a step closer, her voice a pulse. A hush.

Pippa just told me they did.

Pippa's unwell, Margaret said. And what do you mean by "kid"?

Eighteen.

Oh. Well, Margaret said, tapping her ash onto the porch rug, toeing it with her shoe. Malachy Sanders? Are you sure?

As if the problem was not the sex but that he was short and wore his trousers too tight and that his wife, Margaret's oldest friend, had told her his breath was so bad she'd stopped kissing him, and insisted he take her only from behind.

Georgina nodded, sitting down, waiting for her mother to take this burden off her.

And he was—. Georgina hesitated, unsure how to distill what Pippa had told her. He was kind of weird, what he liked to do.

Pippa is prone to exaggeration, Margaret said. You know that.

I believe her.

Margaret tightened her mouth around the cigarette, drawing on it so fiercely the whole length was incinerated.

That was a long time ago, she said, gazing somewhere in the middle distance.

Maybe, but it's why she went away. To New Zealand. Your own daughter, Georgina said, her words spiked with blame. There, she'd said it. Placed it squarely on their mother. But even now, Georgina saw as she watched her, she won't take it.

What are you going to do? Georgina asked.

Do? Margaret stood up and threw her spent cigarette over the railing and into the drift of mint. I'm going to clean the kitchen, she announced. One problem at a time. That's what I'm going to do.

But you must see, Georgina said, putting a leg out to keep her mother there, that this is the reason for everything. What happened to Pippa—

Was not the end of the world, Georgina. I remember Philippa at eighteen. Do you? She wasn't an innocent.

But it was the end of *her* world, Georgina sputtered, trying to keep up with this new savage direction the conversation had taken.

Philippa's fine. She'll be fine. I'm making sure of that.

Margaret stepped over her daughter's outstretched leg and went inside, pulling the screen door open in a single fluid motion that said—better than her words—that she wasn't troubled by this. That it was only the present moment that mattered, not something so far in the past. And Georgina could hear her tidying the plates away, and there was nothing angry or disordered about the way she was clattering them. Georgina heard the water running, and the fridge door opening and closing, and the squeak of the dishwasher's racks . . . methodical, just clearing the mess away like she'd said she was going to. As if that was what mattered.

Georgina went in after her.

Mum, you can't just pretend everything's all right.

I am not pretending, Margaret said, turning to face her daughter.

It was basically *rape*.

And the look that passed across her mother's face took Georgina by such surprise that she found herself unmoored, and trying to understand why her mother had flickered with derision, as if what Georgina had said was so outrageous it was laughable.

I'm going to tell Dad, Georgina said, backing up. And it was only then that her mother snapped to.

No, she said.

Why not?

But Margaret turned back to the dishes as though the matter were settled and there'd be no discussing it, and Georgina knew this was her final word. That to disobey would be to unleash such unpleasantness—

But it was too late for that. Georgina moved through each of the downstairs rooms looking for her father, not sure what she'd say to him, but carried forward by the current of what Pippa had put on her, which had only intensified when their mother had refused to take any of it for herself. *Dr. Sanders.* They'd grown up with that family—Georgina's mind turning to her own son and all the other houses he'd spent nights in. But he was a boy and that was different somehow. Less likely, she thought shakily, even though she'd read things in the paper and knew it happened, but it was always so sensational and athletic—a swim coach or a camp counsellor—but not dumpy old Dr. Sanders, who was always talking about his last vacation or his new car, or the improvements he'd made to his house and cottage. Droning on about the radiant heat he'd put in his floors. Georgina could remember him making her entire family take their shoes and socks off and feel it with their bare feet, encouraging them to lie down and shouting they should press their cheeks to it, lift their shirts and feel how it could warm their backs and soothe tired muscles like a massage. How he liked to lie on it after a bath.

Where was her father? Georgina had come to the living room at the end of the house but there was still no sign of him. She looked out to the white garden, thinking he might be there, and her gaze went to the hedge opening and the city beyond and she felt, suddenly, so unmotivated. Tired. Unsure where to go or what to do, just stuck there staring at the blurry section of her city that showed through the yews—and a fork of blue lake like a serpent's tongue.

Why, she thought, didn't Dr. Sanders go for me? As if that were another failure to add to her list.

Margaret let the water run over her hands and then pressed them into the newly cleared sink, her thumbs hooked into the garburator opening she'd insisted on even though their plumber had staked his reputation on them causing more trouble than they were worth. She pressed the slick black rubber gaskets down and took in the smell of rotting food, trying to clear her head. To focus herself right there, in that moment. It's different, she was repeating softly to herself. *Different, different, different, different . . .* She couldn't go back because she knew there'd be nothing there—no suspicions, no memories, no inkling at all of what had been going on right in front of her. Because she'd only ever drifted through those days, her collages the only thing anchoring her.

Upstairs in their bedroom, David spread his arms and legs out like a starfish, pointing his toes and flexing his wrists and feeling that beautiful ache in his groin and the small of his back, and he was thinking only of how he would do it next. And after that, and after that, and after that . . . *I will just lie here until I'm ready to do her again.*

—

Georgina served them at the table, forking the pasta onto the plates and covering it with the bottled red sauce she'd shaken herbs into to try to make it edible. Despite her shopping trip, the house was low on food again. There was a heap of grated cheddar in the middle of the table, some of it hard and dry. It was the kind of meal they'd had every week as kids but tonight, instead of Jax being there, it was the other girl who was crouched at the far end of the table. Pippa was there too, her first meal at the table since arriving from New Zealand, and Georgina could tell she was trying. She'd changed her clothes and tied her hair back, and was eating her food in small bites.

Where's Jax? Pippa said, looking around.

Out for dinner, Georgina replied. Thinking this was a good sign too; that Pippa was noticing things. Trying to take part.

Who with?

Georgina shrugged, looking to her parents, but of course they wouldn't know. And thinking how familiar this felt, for Jax to have taken off again.

She always has a Plan B, their father said, his fork paused above his plate and his eyes downcast. A contingency, he said. For everything.

Oh yes? his wife said.

You should always have a contingency, he replied.

He was looking at his daughters now, from one to the other, careful not to look at Goldi because he didn't trust himself yet. He suspected his wife had called her to the table as a test. To see if he had the resolve to make this work—to integrate her into their lives without giving anything away.

Right, Georgina said, clearing her throat. Because life's a . . . military campaign?

Exactly, he answered, missing the sarcasm in her voice.

David swallowed his food, straightening his back against his chair, looking at each member of his family like a general assessing their readiness. Their willingness to fight for him. And then his eyes stopped on Goldi and she looked up and smiled. Just a tight, thin-lipped smile, but after that all he could see was her straddling him.

She'd been waiting for him upstairs—ready, already naked—and she'd done everything he wanted her to do, and without all the noise he found so distracting when he did it to his wife.

It's as if, he'd thought to himself afterwards, she's come to me already trained.

Every king, he'd whispered in her ear, *needs his courtesan.*

Andeverycourtesan, she'd whispered back with a finger at his neck, *herfuckingking.*

She's like a wife, he thought now, looking at her there. A more perfect and obedient wife. And he'd not give her up for anything.

What would you do, Georgina continued mildly, dropping more cheese onto her spaghetti and addressing her father, if you were under attack?

Attack?

But it was just an echo, and Georgina could see that his thoughts were somewhere else.

Georgina, Margaret said, asking for the plate of cheese, but Georgina knew she was really warning her to stop.

Goldi, Georgina said instead, following her father's look. Like Golda Meir? Are you the elected leader of your own little country?

The girl kept eating, unaware she was being spoken to, not conditioned yet to respond to the name she'd been given.

229

So, Georgina tried again, seeing that it was beginning to agitate her parents. You're a friend of Pip?

Huh? Pippa looked at her sister, shook her head.

But I thought you said—

Georgina, their mother said sharply.

You told me she was a friend of Pippa, Georgina said, staring hard at her mother.

A little young, don't you think?

It was David, back in charge again, his voice drowning out all the others and suddenly no one cared about the girl and what she was doing there, because this was far more interesting: their father siding with their mother.

Well, Georgina smiled. There's my answer. You circle your wagons.

Goldilocks had found a wrap in the wife's closet. A length of pale blue cashmere she could wind right around herself, which is what she did now that she was alone after dinner, looking at herself in the enormous gilt mirror she'd dragged up to her room in the attic and leaned against the wall. *Totalrockstar*, she thought, turning. Tickled by what she saw. She'd filled the room with a sumptuous wool rug, an upholstered fan-back chair, the large jardinière with a real live trailing plant spilling out, and enough vases and precious bric-a-brac to cover the bedside table, the dresser and the small escritoire against the wall. She'd found sheets and a brocade duvet for the bed, brought up cushions to give the feeling of a harem, and she'd even hung paintings on all the walls so the room looked just like ones she'd seen in luxury magazines. There were enough movable items in that house that she'd be able to redo the space each day, for months, and never run out of objects. Right now the colour blue was the common theme, but next time she might use an animal, or a pattern, or even go around and pick things out by weight. The heaviest, the lightest . . . a thousand combinations she could use. The old man hadn't even noticed. Didn't care. She could do whatever she wanted as long as she kept giving him something in return— and what she gave him was what she gave away anyway. Didn't matter if it was here or there, except that *here*—she spun and giggled—was like a *palace*. Which made her almost like a queen.

Goldi stepped out of her room, into the hall, and went to the broken window. Now that it was dark and the city was lit up like a club—not that ugly toy-town it was during the day with its tiny anonymous citizens—it looked familiar. As if it was applauding her. *Amillionlighters*, she giggled, waving to her audience, posing for her reflection in the remaining glass, opening the wrap and wriggling like a larva. Like the striptease act she'd put herself on holiday from; bump and grind.

This was more like it. This promised more fun. Even the name they'd given her—Goldilocks—sealed it as a fairy tale she could lose herself in forever and ever.

Georgina was climbing the stairs. She paused at the landing outside Pippa's room, knowing she should check on her before going upstairs to bed, but she didn't think she could listen to those allegations of abuse again. Not tonight, after everything else. Even Toronto's lights, sparkling in the distance like a false dawn, were too much, and so she turned away from the huge window at the top of the stairs . . . and maybe it was the silent fact of the girl on the landing above her that brought the image back. Some little sound the girl made that Georgina registered, and so recalled that strange image in the storage room that she'd glimpsed without fully realizing what she was seeing. A knee cap, protruding just barely into her view. Someone squatting? Velvet boots.

Georgina went to that room now and peered inside, tentative, not sure what she wanted to see. Pulled there by the unfinished oddity of it. Grasping for anything that might draw her away from the whole entire shitshow of this family. But there was no one there, and the room—Georgina went in and flipped the light switch and looked around—was just as it always was, a clutter of stuff. Just a closet and big windows that didn't even open, so even the air was second-hand. And that's when she saw it—the collage her mother had been working on. The entire room, she saw now, was like a whirlwind centred on that—on the canvas, and its intentional markings, and how it had been assembled in such a way that the composition was in perfect balance. Not symmetry, Georgina thought, looking down at it, but *balance*. She looked up and saw other sheets of similar paper in stacks about the room—all of them blank—and then the long edge of one sticking out of a portfolio book on a shelf in the closet—and then she saw all the other books. Rows and rows of them. She pulled one down and flipped through it, piece after piece after piece—this passion her mother had allowed herself. Art. Which was what made it so unforgivable. That what her mother had made, for no one but herself, and had stuck away there with all the other detritus of the house, was better than every other thing Georgina had ever done or studied. Better, by far, than the student's work in the gallery downtown. Here, in this otherwise superfluous room, was something essential and genuine.

And it had been here all along.

Truthfully, Georgina had come home not for her sister but for her mother—knowing how a crisis could tip their father into something primitive and raw. It had happened before, and they knew their father's tastes were out of the ordinary, and their mother would suffer for it—but what Georgina realized now was that their mother had never needed any help. These creations spread around her were the earth's crust that all their lives had been laid upon. And there was nothing—nothing—Georgina had ever done that she could compare it to. And this also, Georgina thought as she realized all the hours that must have gone into creating them, must be why their mother had missed what was happening to Philippa. That helped to make it all okay.

Monday

28

At first light, Georgina was woken by Pippa's screaming, and she knew, right away, that her sister was having the baby. She rushed down to her sister's room and saw Pippa dropped against the bed, her knees on the floor, and something—*blood!*— pooling around her.

Dad! Georgina yelled into the near-empty house.

It was all she could do to pull the bedclothes back and lift her sister onto the bed, because the baby was already coming and there was no stopping it.

Where's Dad! Georgina yelled, frantic, running to check her parents' bedroom and then running downstairs, screaming for him to come and help, phoning the paramedics . . . anything so she wouldn't have to go back upstairs to what was happening, because it was the *Death of Marat* and Gericault's heads. It was Goya, a river of gore.

She pressed her hands on the kitchen counter, and tried to slow her breathing.

Dad! she screamed again, emptying her lungs. And then she saw movement out the window—her parents, both of them, closing in on the house.

David had heard the shouts even in the copse, where he'd been seated on the bench in the shade, Goldi's smell still on his fingers, marvelling at his immense good fortune. He'd heard his name and his profession being summoned to the house to help, but he didn't go right away. He waited. Unaccountably, he stood but did nothing else until the garden released his wife, and then he moved. Not a run, and only a touch faster than a walk. His wife was following the driveway, the most direct and unencumbered path, but he went through the garden, stalling the inevitable, because he knew now that the commotion must be the baby. That the house would be filling with anxiety again just when everything had seemed, finally, to be levelling out—and not the same as before, but better. Miles better.

He brushed past Georgina, who was hysterical, circling the kitchen island like a broken toy whose motor won't switch off. He climbed the stairs, the narrow servants' stairs, beginning to feel like one himself, and at the landing didn't pause but walked right in, and what he saw would never leave him because there was his wife, crouched between their daughter's legs, and in her hands was the bloodied head as Pippa pushed it out. It was bedlam but in the centre, Margaret, undeterred by the mess and the smell and the terror of her own child giving birth with no one to help if it all went wrong. And what he felt then was wholly unexpected and sudden: a tenderness so profound it dizzied him. Made everything, except his wife, unsteady and shifting, and he knew that there in front of him, on her knees, was his life's binding. That he owed this woman everything.

David, his wife keened, reaching for him. Oh, David. I shouldn't have.

And they both knew she was referring to the miscarriage she'd admitted to. He took the apology, not as a victory—not as a chance to get and keep the upper hand—but rather as a rebuke for having lost sight of her.

Darling, he said, falling beside her and watching her turn back to the baby as it slid out onto the bed, a viscous mess. And he thought, about his wife: *How exquisite she is, how beautiful. How mine. How exactly what I deserve.*

When the paramedics came, swarming the bed, David and his wife stood to one side against the wall, her back to his chest and his arms wrapped around her like they were a new couple. And David squeezed her then, hard, and whispered a promise in her ear.

I'll never leave you, he said. Never ever.

But Margaret heard it as a threat. As if he'd somehow, because of the intensity of the emotions, divined the entire story of the miscarriage—which was that she'd swallowed so many pills, in an attempt to overdose, her body had jettisoned anything superfluous in order to survive.

We have to take her to the hospital, the paramedics said. It's protocol.

And so they carried Pippa. The servants' stairs were too narrow and the door frames too crooked to get their stretcher through, so the two men—both so young they were almost certainly unmarried and childless—held her in a sheet, an improvised sling, and carried her awkwardly down the stairs and through the butler's pantry and the kitchen, and down the porch steps to the stretcher that hadn't even made it off the driveway. They fussed around her, tucking blankets and securing straps and cranking the mattress so Pippa was slightly elevated, all the carnage out of sight and the baby nestled into her and snuffling. Hadn't even cried yet but no one seemed alarmed, as if the worst was over, and everything from now on was going to be a dream.

Always thought it would be me, Margaret whispered. Leaving the house like that.

She and David listened to the ambulance make its way onto the lane and along the escarpment—the crunch of gravel, and the squeak of branches scraping its sides. Both just standing there, next to each other, unremarkable.

David, she said finally. I have to tell you about Malachy.

It was dark inside the coach house, and cool. Georgina had brought the two black garbage bags filled with the mess from Pippa's room—the bottom sheet, the blankets, even the pillow though it didn't have a drop of anything on it—down the drive to the coach house to be kept until collection day. She'd used two big towels to mop up where Pippa's water had broken, throwing those into a garbage bag too. No one had asked her to do it, but who else was going to? Jax hadn't come home last night and that girl upstairs might not be a guest, exactly, but she wasn't a maid either. And it helped to have something to do.

After she'd dropped the bags into the large bins, Georgina dawdled—picking up some gardening shears, a broken nozzle, a croquet mallet, part of a plastic pull-behind toy. She drifted into the small side room and brushed by the high bench loaded with chemicals, the empty hooks that the gardening tools were supposed to be hanging from, the bundle of chicken wire, the tangle of garden hoses and power cords. This coach house had always felt, even more than the house itself, like a remnant from another era. The locks were black metal boxes attached to the doors below the cold porcelain knobs. The mechanism that drew the heavy main doors back like an accordion's bellows, to allow enough space for two coaches to be backed in side by side, looked like something forged and hammered by a blacksmith. The walls were constructed of limestone mortared together, and the windows were too small to shed light. They'd always seemed, to Georgina, like arrowslits—as though this structure were a barbican. Electricity had been added later, thick knob-and-tube wiring secured to the walls for a single bare bulb in each room to push the gloom back.

Georgina opened the latched door and went upstairs, to where the groomsman would have lived, stepping onto the rough pine floor she and her sisters had painted and repainted with each new club when they were children, and this was their secret meeting place. Roofing tacks shot through the ceiling and they'd all learned to crouch on either side of the ridge line to keep their scalps free of injury. She remembered that now, and ducked. The yellowed lace curtains, the old vinyl couch and chair, the coffee table, the stepstool—everything salvaged from the house, from the occasional purges their mother performed. Entire summers they'd spent up there, jockeying for control, settling arguments by standing in a circle with one bare foot forward until they touched, Georgina raising a brick overhead and letting it fall, the last girl to pull her foot back the winner. *Why didn't we just toss a coin? One potato two potato, eeny-meeny-miny-moe?* They'd argued about almost everything: about what they would name their clubs, about what colour paint they would use—even how to hold the brushes and rollers. But between those confrontations, there must have been long, lazy days of calm. She remembered bike rides, with just the three of them. Spy missions undertaken, sleep-outs where they'd huddled together against some imagined common enemy. Moments when they'd come to one another's rescue, big and small.

And yet, just now, when Pippa had needed them—she'd walked away, and Jax hadn't even shown up. When had it come to this?

The rat droppings, the dirt on the glass, the ragged cobwebs that had taken over now—this, she felt, was what she needed. Not more composure. Not more pianola controlling the tempo of her life, automatic and error-free, its paper roll looping endlessly around the repeating holes of work and family. Not that house down the drive with its comforts, and its people pressing in on her. Philippa had had her baby. What now?

Georgina placed a hand on the tacks. Still sharp. When, she wondered, had the clubs given way to other secrets? *Secrets we kept to ourselves.*

29

Pippa let the baby press her into the thin raft of hospital pillows at her back, its tight body cramped around her breast, the warmth flooding—she could feel it—down from her shoulders and her chest and her back, all focused on that little striving mouth. She was so beautiful. So perfect and so beautiful. The world was suddenly filled with levity, all the darkness of the past few months fled and replaced by this pure delight. She paid no mind to the doctors or the nurses, letting them move her arms and legs around, peer at her, stick her with needles, stitch her up, take her vitals . . . all just background to the majesty of this tiny perfect creature curled against her in that hospital bed.

Leo, Pippa would breathe into the telephone later that night, *you have a daughter now. You have to stop.* No more sex. Or drugs.

Or rock and roll. *I'm coming back, but only then.* The trans-Pacific cable, thousands of fathoms down on the seabed, almost split by the weight of that—because Pippa knew, and remembered, what a man could do to a girl.

When Jax stepped into the room, Pippa and the baby were asleep, and so she sat by the bed and waited. It didn't take long for them to stir, because if they lay on a cushion of innocence, then Jax had come raging in on a tide of sin.

Where've you been? Pippa asked, shifting the baby to her other breast. You look rough.

Yeah, Jax mumbled. Maybe I'll take a shower in that invalid bathroom over there.

Your turn to be sick now, is it?

Jax pulled her sleeves down. Noticing, only now, that she'd missed a button on her shirt.

Where is everyone?

Pippa flicked her eyes to the window, and the cliff face rising up behind the parking garage.

I had her up at the house, she said.

Jax stared at the baby's soft head, trying to picture it, the birth.

The house?

Pippa grinned then, the whole experience suddenly so hysterically funny. Yeah. Beside my bed. And then, well, *on* my bed.

Jax was laughing now too, still giddy from her night on the lake. Everything off-kilter.

Had to carry me down in a sheet.

A *sheet?*

Pippa crying she was laughing so hard, recounting—in gasps—what she remembered of that morning: the cute first responder who'd massaged her feet in the back of the ambulance, Georgina panicking, their father up against a wall and staring—she thought, she said, that he might actually have vomited—and Mum. *Mum.* She got the baby out.

What?

Delivered it.

Mum did?

Yeah, Pippa nodded. For real.

Trust you, Jax said, to take something simple and make it a spectacle.

But where were you?

Out. Jax smiled.

Sex, Pippa said, raising an eyebrow. Because Jax was glowing—life suddenly beautiful for her too. I hope you're being careful, she said, stroking her newborn's back.

I don't even know what you're talking about.

You've been here—what, two nights? Three? Didn't take you long.

Jax shrugged, got up and walked around the bed to the window.

Who was it? Anyone I know?

Who was what? Nobody, and nothing.

Uh-huh.

Jesus. It's not like it's a fucking *reggae club* filled with gigolos, Jax said, turning away from the window, her reaction setting them both laughing again.

It *was* Billy, though. Remember Billy?

Of course I remember Billy, Pippa said. Both of them lost for a moment in that memory of a night when the world had seemed so much bigger than it had eventually turned out to be.

Is he still hot?

Yes, Jax sighed. Still very, very hot.

You always got the best-looking guys.

Get, Jax corrected her. Because I'm still the best-looking girl.

Except for me, of course. Ravishing, even after an emergency birth.

Jax rolled her eyes. You're a baby, she scoffed. A baby having a baby. When I called home, Mum said she was sending George down. Or Dad, maybe? I don't remember.

Hopefully to pick me up. I can't wait to get out of here.

So. Jax sat on the bed. What's her name?

Pippa looked helpless. I never had to pick a girl's name before.

Let me hold her.

Jax took the tightly swaddled baby and lay her along the bend of one arm, pulling her in against her body and laughing at the little mouth searching for a nipple.

She's a good eater, Jax said, putting a finger there for her to latch on to. No Christines or Teresas; they'll just get shortened to Chris or Teri. You need a definite girl's name. A Vanessa. Or a Stacey. Catherine?

I don't know. Maybe a Maori name.

Yeah, you're such a fucking Maori. She's going to be a red-head like you. What about Ginger! Or Ruby? She handed her back then because the baby had started to cry, her mouth suck-ing in air and her entire body spasming with the effort. She's perfect, Jax said, whatever you end up calling her.

Jax had met her husband over a rock pool at the beach. He'd impressed her by naming everything—chitons, limpets, whelks, krill—and she'd replied with similes—the rocks are like promenades, the crabs like advancing infantry. As if together, their understanding might be complete, their two languages combined to make the original one. He'd known all of it—the class, order, family, genus, species—as though he lived inside a diagram, caught between the pages, a tenth edition, everything vetted by the scientific community and nothing left to chance. Was that what bothered her—that he didn't ask for more? She knew he was smart enough—that his mind could hold more than it did—but he didn't seem to care. Even the kayaks, which had been something new they'd discovered together, had become routine and—for him—limiting. When they nosed out of the shallows and left the mangroves she knew he'd paddle straight for open water, disregarding surface breaks that signalled oyster bars and shoals, as if an inch of water didn't matter and he could just glide over it. Or as if he hadn't even considered it. She knew he'd throw a hook in without expecting any bites and he'd wait in his seat while she and the children got out to beachcomb the spindrift islands they came upon, marvelling over finds. It was a workout, that's all it was for him. A chance to get a tan. Was that really all he was?

What she and her husband had shared, Jax realized now, was cowardice. Never having more than what they'd settled for, which was whatever had come to them easily. But now, she thought, as she watched her sister's greedy baby—now she'd gone and done something brave. Her husband? He'd never know. And Billy would only be the first of many more to come.

30

Margaret declared the crisis over. Holding her newest grand-daughter, and making Pippa a restorative cup of tea, she said that it was high time for everyone to go home. Everything—she put the scalding mug down in front of her youngest daughter—had been sorted now. In the morning they should all update their travel plans. She looked from Pippa to Jax to Georgina, daring anyone to contradict her. And she looked at her husband, whom she'd summoned to come and see the new baby, but he was already edging out, back to his unfinished business on the third floor. She knew he hadn't seen any parallels between Malachy and what he was doing with that girl upstairs, because Goldi was a transaction, not a transgression. A professional. And here, anyway, was the best outcome of that fairy tale—keeping David away. He hardly mattered anymore.

Have you named her? Georgina asked.

And Pippa, as if remembering the baby then, reached for her, but Margaret had already turned away and was pacing and rocking because the baby had begun to cry, muffled by Margaret's arm but still audible. All the women in that room knew the baby was hungry, and that the cry would only become more insistent, but they did nothing to make it stop. Pippa, calmly, sipped her tea as if the baby should wait. Laying down boundaries, showing she was capable again, that no one ruled her life but her.

Lucia, she said, looking over at Jax. I'll call her Lucy.

No mistaking that for a boy, Jax said.

And as if, now named, the spell was broken, Margaret passed the baby back and the mood lifted and they all stood where they were, smiling foolishly, as if they'd each been handed an enormous prize. Nothing they'd asked for, but now that they had it—they knew it was going to make everything all right. All of it, just all right.

They drew in, like moths, around that mother and her nursing child, each of them remembering what that was like. A drug. Time slowing to nothing.

Why don't you have a shower, Margaret said when the baby was full and sleeping, lifting it off its mother. You'll feel so much better after a shower, Philippa.

Then she left her daughters there, moving slowly so she wouldn't raise the alarm, although they scarcely paid attention to her anyway because they were sisters—their own tribe—and she knew they'd never had much use for her. She went to the library and nestled into the armchair under the windows, facing the dusty fireplace and the books that were laddered to the ceiling. The rubbish from the stickers was still spread across the desk. It was the last place anyone would think to look for her, because Margaret just needed some time. She cooed, bending her head to that delicious newborn smell, kissing the baby's forehead with her lips parted so she could taste it. Philippa already has enough and this one—she held it more tightly—can be mine. *My baby has come back for me.*

Gave us quite a scare, Margaret said softly, looking down at the baby. Yes, she decided. Wrapped up in its white blanket, face pinched and eyes tight, this one could certainly be a boy.

Margaret untucked the corner of the blanket and began to unwind it like a shroud, working carefully, ready to catch any burial objects that might fall from between its layers. What she needed was the umbilicus so she could add it to the very centre of her collage. It was exactly what she needed to complete the piece. She kept unravelling until she'd bared the pulsing tummy and she put her fingers on the shrivelled stump, tugged it gently just above the plastic clip, but it was still too fresh and pliable to break. She would have to sever it herself. There were scissors in her studio.

She floated through the house as though it was midnight and she was trying not to wake her family. As soon as she turned the light on, she could see that someone had been going through her work. It was all out of order, scattered about like garbage. Even the ones from the cupboard had been brought down and left lying on the floor and across the desk, propped up on chairs and windowsills and against the baseboards. Margaret clutched the baby. Who? But she knew. *That little bitch in heat.*

Margaret backed out of the room, livid, even the presence of the baby not enough to draw her anger down, and she half ran upstairs. The girl's door was open but she wasn't in there, or in the closet, or cowering beneath the cushions or duvet or behind any of the other possessions she'd looted—Margaret could see that now—to decorate the space. Like she owned the place.

Margaret strode across the attic to the other staircase and down to her own bedroom, sure she'd find her there in flagrante delicto with her husband, but it was only David, coming out of the bathroom with a towel about his waist—and she wanted to screech with laughter and belittle him. Point out how old he looked. How his chest sagged and the skin along his sides was loose and pale, and that there was even something pathetic about how he had to grip the towel to keep it up. That nothing about him was lusty or essential.

It's over, she said.

David regarded her coolly, looking from his wife's face to the baby and back up to her face again, the picture steady now. He'd had his small moment of weakness but that was over and he was a leopard again, on the battlefield.

I know, he said. I was there.

The girl, Margaret spat at him. That girl is done.

Oh. Is she?

He slid past the foot of the bed and around to his dressing room, everything about him telegraphing nonchalance, but Margaret knew this technique of his. It was designed to put her off, and she wouldn't have it. Not this time. Not ever again.

Pity, isn't it? he said casually. About that baby being a girl.

He was across the threshold, hand on the door and ready to close it, the space between them so piled high with grievances that his words were almost lost in their accumulated mass. But he knew, from the way she stood motionless and unbreathing, that they'd hit their mark.

Before the family had their supper, Margaret took a tray to Goldilocks, who was up in her room now, stretched out under the covers and sleeping. On that tray was a feast, and all of it laced with the stockpiled chemicals. Enough to sicken, not kill— but enough to make the girl unavailable. For Margaret to show her husband that whatever he had was because of her, and she could take it all away.

Dear, she said, reaching for the rise of the girl's shoulder. Jostling it, maintaining the note of cheeriness she'd practised the whole way up, coaxing. I know you're hungry. She watched as the girl flung an arm out—confirming that she was only motivated by appetites, a beast, pulling the chunk of cake in under the covers to eat, shooting her other hand out to grab pasta. A rumble of obscenities as the bitterness registered on her taste buds, but the sensation only made her reach for more and more, as if the antidote was gluttony. A bigger flavour to mask a lesser one. That it was only the *shell* of the offerings that were repulsive and that like so many other things in her experience, all she had to do was push through the discomfort to get to her reward. She'd tasted worse. Not for a moment did she consider poison.

Margaret shut the door, passed the broken window with a few jagged shards still vibrating in the glazing, and went downstairs. Let the house do the rest, she thought. Let the unforgiving heat build throughout the day. Let that corner room, with its sloped ceiling, become the widening gyre.

Tuesday

31

It was as if they hadn't even moved, Margaret and the girls. Still milling about the kitchen with cups of tea and bits of cake, and the baby in someone's arms and crying. As if it had all just continued without David there, all night. Couldn't they do anything properly? He was already in a foul mood—his evening pleasures having been denied to him, just when he'd begun to settle into a comfortable routine.

Give it here, he said, taking the baby, still in his pyjamas and dressing gown. He would walk it and make it quiet, play the martyr. It wasn't only his wife who was good at that. Before his tea or his porridge or the morning paper even, before any of that, he'd show them how it was done. Out the door and down the drive, remembering the course he'd trodden with the other grandchildren when they were babies and crying and he'd taken them. Conquered them. Down the drive, into the rhodies, around the tennis court and back round to the roses, and again and again for as long as it took. And when that loop got tedious he'd take the path along the perennials to the cliff and the white garden and pool and herbaceous border . . . *my empire*, he thought above the baby's racket, *is vast. A hundred thousand ways I can travel through my realm. And this one*—he shifted the baby to the other side—*weighs nothing. Some of those others had been heavy as lead, but this little thing is featherlight. Hardly there.* He rolled her into his chest, stifling the cries, watching her tiny fists against him, feeling how stiff she was, impressed by her drive to sustain herself. *A fighter. Yes. Girls are always that. And boys? What did he know of them except . . . mine didn't fight hard enough.*

He moved with it to the tennis court. Skirted the edge, around to the roses, a sprawling bush snagging his pyjamas at the knee and scratching his skin. The baby was still screaming, louder than ever. His arms were suddenly heavy and he wondered if this might be the start of a heart attack, trying to concentrate on the pins and needles—which arm? And shooting pain as well? Was he short of breath? And dizzy? A stroke, with the stress he'd been under, wouldn't surprise him at all. And cancer lurking somewhere in his cells was a virtual certainty. But the baby wouldn't let him concentrate. The noise, even smothered by his body, was maddening and someone had left cuttings along the bed's edge, and it made the ground uneven, and it wouldn't be hard to stumble, squashing the breath right out of both of them. He'd sustain an injury. Be knocked unconscious, probably. Might even die. Thinking, suddenly, of Goldi and how unresponsive she'd been. *Like fucking a corpse*, he thought, uneasy, seeing it now for what it was—a prefiguring of his own collapse.

David, resolving not to give in, to let his wife win, to show weakness, to buckle under this problem that had, he thought, been unfairly thrust on him, walked to the farthest reach of his land, as if pressing the very boundaries was all that was needed. To the corner at the cliff where the property lines intersected and, like a shot, the wind coming up from the city and off the lake made the baby catch its breath and stop. Only for an instant, but long enough for David to realize that's all it took—a change of elevation, a sudden wind. And so he propped his arms on the fence's edge to take the burden off them, and the baby, suspended, was so still and quiet and his relief was so immediate that, without intending to, he relaxed his grip just enough that gravity took the dead weight of that baby and pulled, and David, realizing a split second too late, could do nothing to stop it. His panic then was genuine and visceral, and despite his age and all his imagined maladies, he ran for the house. Covering the ground in a mad scurrying gait until he gained the porch, bursting into the kitchen and screaming to the room,

Why'd you give it to me?

Accusatory, back on top.

You gave that baby to *me*.

32

Pippa was out the door before her father finished yelling, running not for the mountain's brow but for the trail at the end of the lane, behind the convent, where she could turn up under the cliff and along the maintenance path she hadn't been on since she was a kid, exploring. The flat, level ground just wide enough for a man and his tools—someone to tighten the massive bolts pinning the metal retaining wall into the limestone of the Canadian Shield; the only thing stopping the whole slab, and the houses on top of it, from crumbling to the road below.

She clawed across the piles of yard waste the landscapers and gardeners had been dropping over the cliff, season after season for years. Each house with a sliding pile of grass clippings and leaves and limbs pruned to a point that knifed her in the arms and legs, and down one side of her face. She should slow down.

Listen for crying. Anything. Up ahead she could see where the cliff curved out of sight beyond the edge of their property and so she knew she must be almost directly below their fence line, nearing where the baby would have dropped, and what she saw wasn't reassuring—so much debris tossed over the cliff, over the years, that the path was obliterated by a false hillside. A shifting pocket-filled unstable slurry of vegetative shit that her parents and their help had been adding to for decades. Like a trampoline, she thought, trying to walk across it, her legs falling through in places and springing back up in others. A baby, hitting this, could've been bounced clear into the trees, or to the traffic one hundred feet below.

Lucy, she called out feebly. Luuuucyyy. Checking the limbs of trees for a body hanging there like refuse from a receding flood. As if the baby, less than a day old, might respond. Might have the awareness to know she'd been thrown away. That this glimpse of the world was all she would ever get.

But Pippa refused to believe that. This girl would be different. Even their father, the despot king, couldn't extinguish her. Even their mother, she thought triumphantly, searching through the brushwood with both hands, couldn't ignore that this girl, born out of strife, would live to lay waste to them all. She was the inheritance they'd been saving for.

And what Pippa found then was a miracle.

Like a paid ticket stabbed on a spindle, the baby had landed on a cut branch from a lilac tree and the wood was holding her there, eyes closed and face relaxed. Pippa recoiled from the impossible doll-like stillness of the swaddling. The blood, where the stick had pierced the baby's side, was pooling at her back, and what Pippa saw, inching slowly forward now, making herself do it, was the alabaster perfection of eternal rest. A baby so peaceful and flawless in the rude crèche of her surroundings that the myth of a son of God born in a stable made sense to Pippa now because anyone, she thought, would die for this. *Even me.* For the shocking innocence of it in the middle of all that wreckage. And when Pippa got close enough for the detritus under them to shift from her weight, she was ready to believe anything.

Pippa! Pip!

It was her sisters, at the fence, shouting down, watching her progress, barely audible over the absolute silence she'd made for herself in her baby's presence. And as she crept forward, the shifting debris must have jiggled the branch just enough to shoot new pain through the tiny body, to tear the skin a little more, rip at the muscle it had grazed next to her rib cage, pinning her there.

Because Lucy began to cry. And Pippa grabbed her up and put her to her breast, which was wet with milk now. Aching to feed her.

Margaret looked down at her husband sitting there, still struggling to breathe, still wild-eyed and dishevelled, but already beginning—she knew the signs—to rearm himself. She'd expected the glacier, she'd hoped for his help, but she had never expected this. That he'd take another one. That despite everything she'd put in place . . .

She would have to hurt him back. She would have to finish him.

—

It had been hours since breakfast and the house, after all the commotion, was still. The baby had been patched up and the police tipped off by the hospital. The policeman stood there and waited for an answer to his question. It was Margaret who spoke first, her children arranged beside her on the driveway like a show of flags. A coalition. David was there too, because where else would he be. The girl was upstairs and vomiting.

He tripped, Margaret said, nodding to her husband. The baby fell. It was, she quavered (her tone believable), a terrible accident.

Even Pippa, back from the ER and holding her mended baby, nodded that this was true because how else to explain what had happened—and what else would this policeman understand? All that mattered now was to get herself and her baby back home, to New Zealand, and any further enquiries would just delay that from happening. Once she was gone, she would never have to come back.

Jacqueline, her mother directed, tell the officer everything.

And so Jax spoke, holding fast to the position that the baby had been saved because of the family's vigilance. Because of their herculean efforts to restore order when all around them, like a thunderbolt, the world was descending into chaos. She knew they were all accomplices and that her report had to free them all from blame, and so she drew herself up and used heroic language steeped in myth to colour the scene and fashion this baby as the second coming; to elevate her to such grand proportions that who could doubt their intentions with a creature so pure and precious as this one was . . . or that attractive family, who'd left their well-appointed and magnificent home to meet this nervous young constable on the crushed gravel of their spectacular grounds? They who were sharing the details of this near tragedy, this private matter, without affectation or disdain. Her performance was riveting.

He snapped his notebook shut and apologized for the intrusion.

I'm a new father too, he said. I know how hard it can be.

As if, somehow, this event was just another domestic oversight due to sleeplessness.

And then there was the scattering: each family member had somewhere else to go.

Philippa, her mother said quietly as she turned to go inside. I've booked our flights. We leave tomorrow. I'm going with you, she said, answering her daughter's look, to get you settled.

Tea, Margaret instructed her eldest daughter then, and Georgina complied without argument because she was floundering, and the familiar ritual would give her something to focus on.

And Jax? Jax was the first to leave. A taxi back to the airport that very night. She knew, better than anyone, when the party was done—and where the next one was about to begin.

Epilogue

It had been months since Georgina had been to the house. Not since everyone, excepting their father, had left. The university was back in session now and she'd been busy with lectures and meetings and student problems, but her mother had called and interrupted that, told her to deliver a message to her father: she was not coming back. This was a message Georgina had relayed before, over the years, and she didn't credit it this time any more than she had on the previous occasions, even though the particular crisis that had precipitated their mother's flight had seemed, at least on the face of it, to have been graver than the others. Her father, she thought mercifully, might need the message softened because there was always the chance—statistically infinitesimal—that this would be the instance when the message proved to be true . . . and it would be she who'd have to deal with the outcome.

Georgina had spoken to her father on the phone more frequently in recent weeks. A sort of rising tide of communication. He called her when he was looking for things—a book, the can opener, the magnifying glass that should be with the dictionary but wasn't—and left clipped messages if she didn't answer, as if he knew that she and her husband and son were screening him. She had the creeping sense that he might be breaking down. In his last call, he'd mentioned retirement as if it were already under way. As if he'd stopped going in for his clinics. Georgina knew that mustn't be right, because surely it would take longer than a few months for him to close his practice down completely. He had staff he'd have to give notice to, and patients he'd have to stop scheduling, and a building and equipment he'd have to liquidate. None of it sounded right. And even if her mother hadn't phoned with her declaration, Georgina would probably have gone up to the house anyway just to check on him, make sure he was still ticking along.

And to her relief, when she entered the lane and the drive, everything looked just the same as it always did. Leaves were only just now budding out, and in the gardens, planted as they'd been to showcase every season, with the leaves gone and the blossoms not yet there, the shapes of things had become paramount. Even the barren trees seemed sculpted by an artist's hand. Made to look like staghorns and fragile gorgonians—something you might chance upon in a fairy tale. The drive had its dappling of light and the house looked fiery in the full sun. It always felt good to come back, especially after an absence, the house always giving the impression of welcoming you. Of being a refuge you could count on. Many lifetimes of memories keeping its walls upright.

Every Easter, like some grand estate, her parents had opened these gardens for a hunt that was attended by other children whom Georgina and her sisters barely knew. Girls and boys that they'd had to race for their milk chocolate and jellybeans, the adults ranged along the terrace coaching them. *Blood sport*, their father called it admiringly, watching the escalating carnage unspool while their mother moved anxiously among the mob of children trying to preserve her swaying beds of alliums from being snapped, and to curtail the trampling of pasque flowers, striped squills, daffodils and rock cress that were so pretty at that time of year. Back when it was still only their mother who fretted about what the bacchanalia would do to the plantings. The ground, Georgina recalled as she slowed her car on the crunching gravel, was often soft from rain, and all the lovely Easter dresses and short pants, by the end of the hunt, were ruined by mud. Great licks of it up shins and across chests where the children had flung themselves under shrubs to fight for the sweets.

It was their father who hid those sweets. Georgina and her sisters would spy him from the upper windows before everyone arrived as he trundled the wheelbarrow along pathways, heavy with chocolate—never any pretense of a magical bunny—and always, somewhere, he would hide a golden egg. A small gilt oval hinged on one side, into which he'd folded a one-hundred-dollar note. He hid it so ingeniously that none of the children could ever find it, and after they tried and failed for what he deemed long enough he opened the search to the seething adults, and Georgina remembered how dangerous that had felt with those heavy bodies careening out of control, and how all the children would flee for the safety of the tennis court to watch their parents rage beyond the chain-link fence. But one uncommon year,

Georgina recalled as she stopped her car, stricken by the memory, it was she who'd found the golden egg hidden high in the crook of that hawthorn tree there, nestled among three-inch thorns and new blossoms. It had glinted at her in the weak afternoon sun as she'd shimmied up the trunk, breaking spikes off until her palms and wrists were striped red but determined to get it, just barely reaching the egg with her fingertips and knocking it loose. Fumbling then, both she and the prize falling to the ground, where she lost it in the circular planting of marsh marigolds—just long enough for a boy, older and bigger than her, to pounce on it.

Mine! he'd cried in victory, dropping his shoulder and all his weight against her outstretched arm and splintering it into the ground, her fingers wrapped around the gold orb and refusing to let go.

Georgina had worn a plaster cast for a month—a comminuted fracture of her right humerus—but more memorable was her father's approval that she'd kept her grip. *For fighting*, he'd announced proudly as he'd carried her to the house from the base of that tree, *for what was rightfully yours and threatened.*

Georgina had basked in the adulation of that father—her golden, unassailable father—the egg and its contents pressed into her stomach, folded into the sling of her ten-year-old body as it hung lightly from her father's arms as if it was just where it had always belonged, because she was struck by how effortless his movements were. Her father didn't groan at the added weight, or run short of breath. He *strode*. The crowd *parted*. She was his.

—

As she'd done countless times before, Georgina went into the kitchen and called out for anyone home, for her father, and then opened the refrigerator to scan it for something tasty. Always hungry in that house. The fridge was filled, every inch of it, with take-out containers. Styrofoam, cardboard, clear plastic clamshell packaging—every ethnicity the city harboured. Their sides were stained overflows of red and green and mustard yellow, and even with all the sauces congealed she could smell coriander and oyster sauce and cumin. Strange, because her father maintained that spices only ruined the taste of food—that a good gravy was all you ever needed. The door in her hand rattled with beer bottles and ginger ales. When had her father started to drink those?

She shut the fridge and looked around and saw, now, that every surface was a mess. And not just dirty dishes and opened tins and food scraps—although there were a multitude of those—but the entire contents of cupboards emptied and piled across tables and countertops, even the floor. A vomitous spewing of possessions, picked over and dumped as if someone had been searching for something particular and these were the spoil piles. The slag heap. And every room Georgina walked through, stunned by the shambles, was the same—everything hidden had been brought out and subjected to light. But where was her father? And what had happened to the cleaning woman who came every other week? She would never have let it come to this. Georgina had always thought it was her father—not her mother—who had kept the household neat with his demands, but this devastation put that into question.

She went from room to room, calling out. Her father's car was outside, so she knew he had to be there somewhere. Upstairs, it was even worse. Every one of the beds unmade and every bathroom floor damp and littered with used towels, and the lights were all turned on as if someone wanted to make it eternally day inside. Keeping watch—but for what? Her old bedroom, which should have been dark because its curtains were pulled shut, was illuminated by its sconce and both bedside lamps. Even the closet light had been left on. But there was no sign of her father—unless you counted the tornado of possessions. His room was no different, and the sewing room was piled high with linens and the bed in Pippa's room had been tossed, and their mother's hidden room beside that had its door hanging from a hinge, and the frame splintered at the lock where someone had broken it in. Inside, however, it seemed untouched because that room had always been a mess. In fact, Georgina noticed, it had been somewhat tidied. The collages were back on their shelf. She knew her mother would have done that before she'd left—collected and filed them chronologically and—she looked back at the ruined door—locked them away so no one could have them.

Georgina smiled then, the idea coming to her like a shot as she looked at the neat row of books, thinking that here was something she could do better than anyone. And a reason for her mother to come back.

She took the first two portfolios down and began to pull the individual sheets out. This work was best curated thematically, she was certain of that. Forgetting about her father, she began to arrange the collages so they'd hang for best effect. She spread them out across the room, stood back to look, rearranged them . . . these were her mother's most recent ones. The events were still in Georgina's memory and she let that guide her, putting it within the framework of all her years of scholarship, until it was perfect—perfect and provocative—and then she took the tub of glue from the desk and began to smear it across the walls. She papered those raw canvases over all the walls on the second floor. She pasted them over Rembrandts and da Vincis and Caravaggios—these pieces of her mother's there now, instead of hay fields and piazzas and portraiture. She glued them onto windowpanes and doors, and onto the wallpapered expanses between prints. Her mother might have started the work, but it was Georgina who was completing it by pulling it together and showing how it was, in fact, a much larger narrative and not confined to just that house and that family. Teasing out its links to the whole long sweep of art from ancient times. And Georgina didn't stop until she'd curated both books and created in that house an exhibition that swirled through every room and up every staircase and even, in the attic, across the ceiling like a plume. Like a torrent looking for an exit. Working in a fever until she came to the corner room, and then she stopped. For here she had found the only room in the entire house that was kept neat and tidy. It was the room the stray girl had been in, she remembered, and she paused at the open doorway to take it in.

The room was choked with furniture and *objets d'art*, but everything had been placed so carefully that the effect was of an intentional layering, rather than a jumble. Like a perspectival field—the Teatro Olimpico with its *trompe l'oeil* panels vanishing to a point. And that point, in this room, was the bed. Its cover taut and its corners tucked, and a mass of pillows propped against the headboard in diminishing bands so that the ones nearest the foot of the bed were little more than a doll's cushions. The room seemed to have siphoned all the warmth from the rest of the house because the air inside was hot, despite its being early spring and the weak sun failing now as night came. But what was even stranger, Georgina noticed when she stepped over the threshold, was the lack of anything personal. That it could be so perfectly set up, so *inhabited*, but that there should be no clothes or half-read books or forgotten papers lying around.

It's a room made up, she thought, in the *hope* of a visitor. A guest room at the ready. But who would want to stay up here, when there were larger and better rooms on the second floor?

It was through the broken third-floor window that she spied him, finally. Standing at the cliff's edge with his arms raised, the low cloud mist that was covering the city pushing at his feet like ocean foam. He was wearing his dressing gown loose like a robe, but there was nothing revelatory or exultant about him. He was just an old man who'd wandered up against a fence, confused, bedraggled, unsure what to do. He looked frail, as if he needed rescuing. Pitiable.

And so Georgina started down, confident that her solution would please him. Greedy to tell him what it was.

David, as he did each day, stood at the cliff's very edge to look out over his city, believing that the girl would see him. That there was something about him that would glimmer and catch her eye, and she would come back. But today there was a fog right to his feet and he couldn't see anything, and that was ruining it. He'd tried imagining that what stretched before him was an immense drift of snow, and that her treachery would stand out against it like a fresh kill and there'd be no hiding, and then his sovereignty would be restored and he'd be king again ... But it wasn't quite right for snow. It just looked like ordinary ground, and this fence just a partition between neighbouring yards. Not lofty, or a pinnacle . . . just ordinary. Ugly and ordinary. No affirmation of a realm.

She had left in broad daylight like a tinker, her stolen wares gathered in stolen bags that she pulled behind her. So heavy he'd watched the rut she carved in the driveway, and thought she'd never get through the potholes and down the lane. That the handles would break or the fabric tear, or her arms be pulled loose and her ankles shattered by the effort to keep dragging forward. That she'd have to return and seek help, and that all he had to do was to stay where he was and wait. *Goldilocks.* She *was* golden, but he knew now that he should have locked her up. *That* was where he'd gone wrong. His wife had known what to do . . . if only he'd paid attention. If only—he slammed both hands down onto the fence spikes until the pain made his arms weak—his household hadn't been so riddled with betrayal.

Georgina descended through the wondrous thing she'd made of the inside of the house, the walls alive now, and she passed through the living room and out to the terrace. The door swung easily on its jamb, the colder temperatures letting the whole building contract just enough to make its skin porous. The summer furniture was still there, its cushions piled with leaves. It was dusk now, but the gravel path arrowed through the white garden and under the pruned evergreen archway like phosphorescence and she could see there, framed perfectly, a single highrise apartment piercing the clouds that were laid across the city. Next year would be her sabbatical year, and what Georgina saw in that building was power, thrust, velocity. The walls of the house flipped inside out. She could curate and promote the remainder of her mother's work. Put together a monograph, bring her back, mount a show. Create a demand and put her mother to work. The coach house, she thought, following the fence line to where her father was gripping it, could be a gallery. *The university can fall away and I'll never have to go back to it.* This could be, she thought, everything I've ever wanted. *Mine.* The house was just a start. It would be the living museum of an artist's life. It was the route you'd take to arrive at the gallery where everything else—and there were still books and books of it—would be for sale. And somewhere, her mother, producing more.

Dad, she said, standing next to him to deliver the message. She told me she's not coming back, but I've found a way to bring her back and keep her here. Come and see what I've done.

He'd turned then and was watching her—this eldest daughter—walk the long way back to the house, around the terrace and past the perennial border. She was walking slowly, waiting for him to catch up.

A *way to bring her back?* His mind always on Goldilocks.

She was running the palm of one hand along the top of a yew hedge he'd clipped as a perimeter, and for one giddy second he thought she might enter the topiary, drop to her knees and crawl. And he would follow her. He would.

Acknowledgements

Much love and gratitude to the following people: my fellow writers—John Griswold, Glen Retief, Carissa Neff, Ed Tarkington, Matt Bondurant, Jane Springer, Cynthia Barnett— for their edits, encouragements and introductions; my friends Caroline Raye, Amy Hudson, Carrie Westmark—for their general wickedness; and Bob Shacochis—for all of the above, and more. Elisabeth Schmitz at Grove Atlantic for her early confidence in me, Katie Raissian at Grove Atlantic for her continued support and perceptive edits, and Nicole Winstanley at Penguin Canada for her enthusiasm and sheer brilliance. Shaun Oakey for his copy-edits, and Terri Nimmo for this stunning cover. My agent, Gail Hochman, for her unfailingly good advice.

And to my family, especially my parents . . . *amor est vitae essentia*. Thank you.